Hello!

Knowing that *Fortune Cookie* would be the last in my Chocolate Box series has been hard; of all the books, it has been the toughest, yet the most satisfying, to write. I guess I just didn't want to let go of my characters and say goodbye to Tanglewood, but I hope the final story will make you smile!

When Jake Cooke gets himself into serious trouble, he runs away to find the half-sisters he has only just discovered in the hope that they can help him save his family from disaster. Will Cookie find the answers he's looking for . . . or perhaps find something more important still? You'll have to read his story and see!

Make yourself a smoothie, sit in the sunshine and soak up the very last adventure at Tanglewood; I think you'll love it. And if you really can't bear to let go of the Chocolate Box world, check out my new book *The Chocolate Box Secrets*, out now . . . Find out the sisters' style secrets, fab recipes and fun ideas, and bring a little Tanglewood cool into your life!

See you soon,

 xxx

Cathy Cassidy

FORTUNE 'COOKIE'

the
chocolate box
~~girls~~ boy

PUFFIN

PUFFIN BOOKS

UK | USA | Canada | Ireland | Australia
India | New Zealand | South Africa

Puffin/Penguin Books is part of the Penguin Random House group of companies
whose addresses can be found at global.penguinrandomhouse.com.

puffinbooks.com

First published 2015
This edition published 2016
006

Set in Baskerville MT by Palimpsest Book Production Limited, Falkirk, Stirlingshire
Printed and bound in Great Britain by Clays Ltd, Elcograf S.p.A.

A CIP catalogue record for this book is available from the British Library

ISBN: 978-0-141-35185-8

www.greenpenguin.co.uk

Penguin Random House is committed to a
sustainable future for our business, our readers
and our planet. This book is made from Forest
Stewardship Council® certified paper.

Thanks . . .

To my fab family, as always . . . Liam, Cait and Cal,
Mum, Joan, Andy, Lori and the whole clan, near and far.
Thanks to my brilliant friends Helen, Sheena, Jessie, Lal,
Fiona, Magi, Mel, Mary-Jane, Janet, Di, Denise and
everyone else who keeps me (almost) sane with laughter,
hugs, chocolate, chat, parties and adventures.

Thanks to Annie, who sorts out my tours so well; Ruth,
my fab PA; and Martyn, who sorts the scary numbers stuff.
Hats off to Darley, the best agent ever, and his team who
are always amazing. Thanks to my wonderful (and patient)
editors Amanda and Carmen who stepped in with wise
words and an adopted llama (yes, really) when I needed it,
and to Sam and her team who did copy-edits in record
time. Hugs to Sara, the best designer ever, and to Carolyn,
Julia, Jess, Tania and the whole Puffin team.

A special shout-out to Evie F. who won a mention in
the story in a comp for the awesome charity It's Good 2
Give (they help children with cancer and their families;
check them out – they need all the help they can get!).
Hope you have fun finding your name, Evie!

Last but not least, thanks to all of YOU, my awesome readers who've been with me every step of the way with this series and make all the hard work worthwhile. And don't worry – there are more books in the pipeline, promise!

RUNAWAY

My mobile buzzes a quiet alarm at four in the morning, and
I push the duvet off and sit up, still wearing my jeans and
T-shirt. My little sisters look like they're asleep when I peer
over the edge of the bunk, but although I'm really careful
as I climb down the ladder, I'm clearly not quiet enough.

Maisie opens her eyes and looks right at me, stricken.

'Shhh!' I whisper. 'Go back to sleep. I'm just going to the
loo.'

But Maisie isn't stupid. I don't usually go to the loo in
the middle of the night, especially not fully dressed and
carrying a rucksack. I see the shine of tears in her eyes, but
I pretend not notice. I want to reach over and ruffle her
hair, tell her it will be OK, but I daren't. That would scare
her even more, and be proof that I was saying goodbye.

'Shhh,' I whisper. 'Don't tell. I'll call you, I promise.'

'Cookie, please don't go . . .' she whispers, but I raise a finger to my lips and she trails away into silence.

I tuck the quilt round her and slip out of the door.

In the living room, Mum is asleep on the sofa bed, the duvet pulled over her head. The flat smells weirdly of damp carpet, washing-up liquid and joss sticks. I step into the little hallway and open the door as quietly as I can, then close it softly behind me. My footsteps sound hollow on the uncarpeted wooden steps as I creep down the stairs and let myself out of the front door; then I am free, stepping into the cool air of an early summer's morning as the dawn light begins to wash through the gloomy streets.

I pause for a few moments to scrawl a few words on the plate glass window of the Chinese restaurant next to the front door; I write the words in letters half a metre high, etched in scarlet lipstick stolen from my mum. She'll be mad about that, but luckily I won't be hanging around to face the flak.

I take a deep breath, check the rail ticket in my pocket and start to walk.

I don't look back.

1

BEFORE

Tanglewood House
Wood Lane
Kitnor
Somerset

Dear Jake,

You don't know me, and this is going to sound slightly
crazy, but hear me out. I have recently found out some
shocking and amazing news about my dad, who's kind of
loaded and now lives in Australia. It turns out that he
had an affair with your mum, like about fourteen years
ago or something, and that makes you my half-brother. I
know, awesome, right?

I am almost sixteen and my name is Honey Tanberry.

I have twin sisters, Skye and Summer, who are fourteen; and a younger sister, Coco, who is about to turn thirteen. So you actually have four half-sisters. There is even a stepsister, Cherry, but I am not sure she actually counts, so we'll just say four for now. This might be a massive shock for you – it was to me – but I am very curious to meet you and find out more about you. Family is important, especially when your dad turns out to be a bit of a let-down, like our dad has.

I haven't actually told my sisters about you yet, as it's quite a bombshell and I am not sure how they will take it. I don't think my mum knows either. So if you have any bright ideas for breaking the news to them, please let me know.

I look forward to hearing from you soon,

Best wishes,
Honey Tanberry

When that first letter arrived, I hadn't believed it. I thought it was some kind of elaborate hoax, like the time Mum got an email saying a distant relative had died unexpectedly in the jungles of Borneo and if she would just reply giving her bank details, a settlement of £500,000 would be paid into her account.

'Is this for real?' I'd asked when she showed me.

'No, Jake, it's just spam,' Mum had said sadly.

It was a different kind of spam from the tinned meat we got at the food bank two years ago, of course. It wasn't mottled pink meat that tasted of rubber, but a hoax, a wind-up, a trick to get Mum's bank details and swipe all her cash.

'Good luck to them with that,' she'd said. 'I am all of seventy-five pence in credit right now. If they need it that badly, they can have it.'

So, yeah, that first letter from Honey Tanberry . . . I thought it was spam.

The letter told me that I might be surprised to learn that I had four half-sisters and a stepsister who I knew nothing about, plus a no-good dad living in Australia. I already knew I had a no-good dad, because Mum had told me often enough; he'd done a vanishing act when he heard I was coming along. As for the sisters, that was nothing to shout about; I already had two, Maisie and Isla, aged nine and five, and they could be annoying enough as it was.

Maybe that first letter was spam, maybe it wasn't; I didn't much care. I scrunched it up and chucked it into the bin.

The second letter came four months later, fizzing with

❁❁❁❁❁❁❁❁❁❁❁❁❁❁❁❁❁❁❁❁❁❁

enthusiasm as if I hadn't blanked the last one. Honey Tanberry was clearly a girl who couldn't take no for an answer. She told me that her family lived in some rambling Victorian house by the sea in Somerset, that I was welcome to visit any time.

Get lost, I'd written back. *I don't believe you. Plus, I have two sisters already. Why would I want more?* It was a short letter, but to the point. I figured that was the only way to shut her up. I didn't know what she was after, but I was wary; it was a scam, it had to be.

Months later, the third letter turned up with photos of the sisters attached. I'll admit that grabbed my attention. They looked like me – or I looked like them, except for the one with almond eyes and blue-black hair tied up in anime bunches, and according to the letter she was the stepsister anyway. The others, though; they looked enough like me to stop me in my tracks.

Fair hair, blue eyes, regular features. One of them had a dreamy look about her, another had a cheeky lopsided grin, one looked sad and lost, and the eldest one looked defiant and dangerous – like she might just explode at any moment. I had seen all those expressions reflected back at

4

me at various times from the cracked mirror in the bathroom, and now they stared out at me, eerily, from a random batch of photographs.

Five beautiful teenage sisters – well, half-sisters, anyway – which is exactly what Maisie and Isla were too. Their dad, Rick, was a bricklayer from Manchester. I used to wish he was my dad, back when we lived there, but that was before he started drinking too much. He lost his job; Mum lost her patience. She left him and vowed she'd never fall for another man again; they were nothing but trouble.

'Not you, Jake,' she'd said at the time. 'Obviously. You're different.'

But I wasn't all that different. I was struggling at school by then, winding up the teachers, breaking rules, damaging school property. 'Nothing but trouble, that boy,' I heard one teacher say in the same despairing tone my mum had used.

I wasn't sure if it made me proud or ashamed.

We left Rick two years ago. Gran sent Mum the money for tickets and we packed our bags and took the train to London.

Mum decided to take us on a sightseeing tour of London before heading to Gran's place. It was our last taste of freedom, she said; we trundled around the city on an open-topped bus and gawped at Nelson's Column and the Tower of London. My little sisters waved at Buckingham Palace as we rattled past, and Mum told them she could see the queen waving back out of one of the upstairs windows.

We jumped off the sightseeing bus in Chinatown. There was a big arching gate painted red and jade, and we went underneath; it was like stepping into a whole different world. The shops sold strange things we'd never seen before, like dried fish and velvet slippers, fat Buddha statues and little model cats painted red and gold with their arms in the air, which Mum said were symbols of good luck.

'Pick a restaurant,' Mum said, and Maisie and Isla pointed at the nearest one, which was called The Paper Dragon and had all these paper puppets of Chinese dragons hanging in the window. We went in and ordered egg foo yung, mushroom chop suey and spring rolls, which was what we always used to order back in Manchester when Rick wanted a takeaway.

They took a long time to arrive, though. It looked like we had picked a dud restaurant. A tidal wave of discontent

❁❁❁❁❁❁❁❁❁❁❁❁❁❁❁❁❁❁❁❁❁❁❁

was mounting around us, cold and ominous. People were not happy. One man demanded to see the manager.

In the end the manager did appear, hot and flustered, with an apron tied over his smart suit. He carried our egg foo yung, mushroom chop suey and spring rolls on a tray.

'Our waitress has just walked out,' he explained, apologetic, setting the food down a little haphazardly. 'The other one has called in sick. It's all a bit crazy here today.'

All around us, customers were grumbling, scowling, demanding to know where their food was.

The manager shrugged. 'I only have one pair of hands. Give me a chance!'

That's when Mum pushed her food aside, got up and marched into the kitchen. She reappeared moments later with dinner plates balanced all along her arm and a smile a mile wide, chatting to a table of surly businessmen as she dished up their order. I don't know what she said, but she turned their scowls to smiles all right.

Maisie, Isla and I ate our food while Mum waitressed, and the tide of gloom and anger lapping at the tables of The Paper Dragon ebbed away. We stayed at our corner table all evening, Maisie and Isla occupied with colouring

❀❀❀❀❀❀❀❀❀❀❀❀❀❀❀❀❀❀❀❀❀❀❀

books and pens and an endless supply of complimentary ice cream. I just listened to my iPod and watched the world going by outside the restaurant window.

This place was very different from the run-down estate we'd lived on with Rick. Nothing much ever happened there, but Chinatown was colourful and bright and loud and lively. As darkness fell the streets lit up, and it seemed like anything and everything was possible. Chinese families came and went, getting on with life; a gaggle of girls in prom dresses spilled out of a stretch limo and skittered into the restaurant across the street; a party of tourists trailed past, following a guide with his umbrella held high in the air. One stopped and took a photograph through the restaurant window, and Isla laughed, put out her tongue and waggled her fingers behind her ears.

By closing time, Mum had a new job – and the offer of a flat above The Paper Dragon.

'This must be my lucky day,' the manager kept saying. 'Alison Cooke, you have saved my skin!'

He gave us a dish with four golden-brown fortune cookies in it, the shells folded in on themselves to conceal their secret messages.

❀❀❀❀❀❀❀❀❀❀❀❀❀❀❀❀❀❀❀❀❀

'Ooh, fortune cookies!' Maisie squealed. 'Like your name, Jake!'

For as long as I could remember, my nickname had been Cookie. Rick had started it, and the kids at school carried it on. It didn't matter which school, either; that nickname followed me around like a shadow that was stuck to my shoe.

'Yeah,' I said. 'How cool.'

We broke the cookies open and fished out the fortunes inside.

'The rough times are behind you now,' Mum's read.

'The time is right to make new friends,' Maisie's said.

'A fresh start is just round the corner,' Isla's insisted.

Mine just said, 'Soon life will become more interesting.'

It wasn't the best fortune in the world, but it turned out to be true. We moved into the flat above the restaurant that night, sleeping on the floor under borrowed blankets. The next day, Mum took out a loan so she could pay rent and a deposit for the flat to Mr Zhao, the manager and owner of The Paper Dragon, and buy some furniture. She chose a second-hand sofa bed, beanbags, a small table and a set of bunks. Maisie and Isla shared the bottom bunk and I

❀❀❀❀❀❀❀❀❀❀❀❀❀❀❀❀❀❀❀❀❀❀

had the top one; Mum slept on the sofa bed.

'It's temporary,' she explained. 'We'll get a few home comforts once I've managed to pay off the loan and save some of my wages, but this will do for now.'

By the time we finally went over to see Gran in Bethnal Green, we'd already been in the flat for a week and Mum was working afternoon and evening shifts in the restaurant. Maisie, Isla and I started school a few days later and that was that; a new life, as if Manchester had never existed.

The flat was damp and scabby, with peeling paint and bare MDF flooring that wobbled when you walked on it, but there were no rows here, no tiptoeing around trying not to get on Rick's nerves. I had to babysit when Mum was working, but we bought a second-hand TV and DVD player and Gran came over some evenings and chilled out with us. I got very good at making beans on toast, mushrooms on toast, scrambled eggs on toast, and there was always leftover food from The Paper Dragon.

We scrubbed the flat from top to bottom, bought a few tins of paint to hide the dirt and mould on the walls and the woodwork, threw down a carpet offcut in the living room. I taught myself to put up shelves. And Chinatown

. . . Chinatown was epic. It was crazy, cool, full of life. I loved it.

So, yeah, when that first letter from my half-sister arrived, forwarded on from Gran's, I genuinely didn't much care. I had a life, I had a family, and that was enough. I was OK.

When the second letter turned up, something began to niggle, to tug away at my curiosity. The letters had made me question things. I'd always known Rick wasn't my dad, but I barely knew anything about my real dad, and a little part of me began to wonder.

After the third letter had arrived, I'd asked Mum to tell me about him. I wasn't about to be fobbed off with the old story that they'd both been too young, that he was scared at the idea of being a dad and decided to disappear. I wanted details.

'Why now?' she wanted to know, tired from a long shift in the restaurant.

'Why not now?' I countered, and Mum had sighed and shrugged.

'He wasn't much of a dad,' she said, frowning. 'We're better off without him.'

❀❀❀❀❀❀❀❀❀❀❀❀❀❀❀❀❀❀❀❀❀❀❀

'But who *was* he?' I persisted. 'How did you meet?'

I had the latest letter folded in my pocket. Honey, my scammer/sister told me that Mum had been a junior member of the sales team in the office where her dad, Greg Tanberry, worked. It looked like Mum had had an affair with a married man. If that were true, it was hardly surprising she'd been sketchy with the details.

'We worked together,' Mum told me vaguely. 'A long time ago. He was my boss. I thought it was serious; he clearly didn't. There's no sense in raking all this up again, Jake.'

'What was his name?' I asked.

She hadn't wanted to tell me. She stalled and blustered and tried to wriggle out of it, but I said that this was my dad we were talking about, that I had a right to know.

'His name was Greg,' she admitted then. 'Greg Tanberry.'

I wondered if everything else in those letters might be true too.

You might be my sister, I wrote back that time. *But you won't want a brother like me, trust me.*

The fourth letter came with a train ticket that was valid for a month and an invitation to come and stay at Tanglewood House.

12

Let me know when you are planning to arrive, Honey had written. *I still haven't told the others about you, but they're going to be so amazed to meet you, I promise!*

Don't hold your breath, I'd written back.

I used a drawing pin to skewer the train ticket to the wall, just above my fortune cookie prediction: 'Soon life will become more interesting.'

I didn't realize then just how true those words would be.

Soon Life Will Become More Interesting!

STD
MAY 2015
FROM
LONDON
TO
EXETER

SGL
2878
£55·00
ANY ROUTE

2

I try very hard to forget that fourth letter. OK, so finding out about my dad could be cool – I won't say I'm not curious about him. I'm only human. I have questions. Do I look like him? Act like him? Does he have a fast car and a jet-set lifestyle?

I like to imagine he does, if only to liven up the grim reality of life in the flat above The Paper Dragon. Before the letters, I barely gave my real dad a thought; now I am intrigued. Does he ever think about me? Maybe not, and if he does he probably doesn't imagine me on my knees in a bathroom where the walls are flecked with mould and the flooring has an ominous crack that squeaks whenever I lean on it, washing my favourite jeans in the bath with washing-up liquid.

It's not a regular hobby of mine, but our washing machine broke six months ago and today we don't have cash for the launderette, and I happen to want my jeans for tomorrow. I am meeting my friends, Harry and Mitch, to see if we can get into a gig for a band called The Thrash Penguins. Harry's big brother is in it, so he might be able to convince the doorman to sneak us on to the guest list, and Harry says there will be loads of cool girls there.

I swish the jeans around again. There's a big soy-sauce stain on one leg from yesterday's shift at The Paper Dragon, where a wodge of leftover chicken noodles spilled all over me as I was stacking the dishwasher. I am working part-time there, because it's the summer holidays and I want to earn some cash. Mr Zhao is grumpy and doesn't pay much, but it's something.

The soy-sauce stain is stubborn, and I have to use the nail brush and loads of washing-up liquid just to get it to fade a little bit. Once the jeans are looking better, I make the most of the soapy water by dumping the entire contents of the laundry basket into the bath and churning up the water to swirl everything around. The bath is filled with white foam and bubbles, with the occasional stripy sock drifting by.

❀❀❀❀❀❀❀❀❀❀❀❀❀❀❀❀❀❀❀❀❀❀❀❀

'Cookie!' my littlest sister Isla yells from the living room. 'Maisie's being mean to me!'

'I'm not!' Maisie shouts back. 'It's Isla. She's got my library book and she won't give it back!'

It is typical of my sisters to embark on World War Three when I am up to my armpits in soapy water. They have a knack for knowing when you've taken your eye off the ball. Suddenly an unearthly roar erupts and Isla is howling and Maisie is yelling, and I sigh and abandon the bathtub-washing. Babysitting my little sisters is a full-time job; they tend to go stir-crazy stuck in the flat, but I'm working in half an hour and it's too late to take them out now, even if I wanted to. Mum is working a long shift from midday to seven, but Gran will be here soon to keep an eye on the girls while I'm working.

'*Cook-eee!*' Maisie shrieks. 'Do something!'

I stomp into the living room. Isla hurls her arms round my waist, sobbing, while Maisie holds up the disputed library book, which looks like it has been through a small explosion. Torn and crumpled pages are scattered about the living room.

'Isla, no!' I scold. 'Library books are special – you can't just rip them up when you get upset!'

'It's a *stupid* book!' she protests.

'It's a broken one now,' I point out, peeling her arms from round me. 'How would you like it if Maisie did that to your books?'

Isla scowls. 'I hate her,' she says in a small, trembly voice.

'Well, I hate *her*,' Maisie counters. 'She is so annoying! I was reading quietly, and now look what she's done!'

'I just wanted her to *play* with me!' Isla sobs.

I sigh. Sometimes I think I might go for a career in world politics, because it seriously cannot be much tougher than keeping the peace between these two.

'Nobody hates anybody,' I say, rolling my eyes. 'C'mon, both of you, wipe those eyes. How about I make some cheese on toast and put the *Frozen* DVD on? Now, are you going to say sorry to Maisie and pick up all this paper?'

Isla mutters a grudging apology and starts picking up the torn pages. I smooth one or two of them out to see if I can do a repair job with Sellotape, but there are too many big chunks missing. Anyone trying to read this particular copy of *Charlie and the Chocolate Factory* will have to invent most of the story as they go along.

We sit down together to eat cheese on toast, and my

phone bleeps with a message from Gran to say that one of the underground lines has been closed and she's running half an hour or so late.

No worries, I text back.

I'm due at work in five minutes, but if I leave the girls watching that *Frozen* DVD they're likely to be spellbound for hours. I've just put the film into the player when I hear a squawk of joy from the bathroom; Isla, washing the crumbs from her fingers, has discovered the bath full of washing. Within minutes, she is dumping in two mangled Barbies and the rest of the washing-up liquid.

'What's all that?' Maisie wants to know. 'What were you trying to do?'

'The washing,' I say. 'No cash for the launderette.'

'It's like something from a cartoon,' she observes, as we watch Isla splashing gleefully. 'Bubbles everywhere!'

'Let her play for a bit,' I say. 'Watch her, and when she gets bored tell her that the *Frozen* DVD is all set to play – you just have to press the button. Gran will be here any minute, OK?'

'OK,' Maisie agrees.

'Cool. Gotta run; will you be all right?'

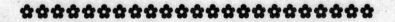

Isla reaches over to her sister and dabs a blob of foam on to her nose, and the uneasy truce melts into giggles at last, and I slip away quietly while the two of them are flicking bubbles around. The bathroom will probably be a mess by the time Gran arrives, but at least it will be clean – and she can wring out my jeans and hang them over the bath to dry.

I run down the stairs and round to the restaurant. The kitchen is hot and steamy; Chang and Liu, the cooks, work at the speed of light, knives flashing, woks sizzling, pans bubbling, chatting the whole time.

I wave at them and grab a clean apron, glancing through the swing doors at the restaurant. It's busy, as always, and Mum looks across and smiles at me. She is dressed in her work uniform, a black silk cheongsam dress with a mandarin collar and gold embroidered dragons and vines; as I watch, she sets down dishes of dessert on one of the central tables, chatting easily. Mum has totally turned things round for The Paper Dragon; Mr Zhao is always telling her she's his lucky charm, but sometimes lately when I look at her she seems tired, even a little sad.

She works too hard, too many shifts; it's taken her two

❀❀❀❀❀❀❀❀❀❀❀❀❀❀❀❀❀❀❀❀❀

years to pay off that loan and get us out of debt, but we're still pretty skint. Life for Mum isn't easy, I know.

'Come on, Cookie,' Mr Zhao says briskly, bustling into the kitchen to pick up two dishes of wonton soup. 'Stop dreaming; start working!'

I load the dishwasher, switch it on and turn my attention to the big pans and woks in the sink. Mum comes in carrying a trayful of dirty dishes; she dumps them down and moves on to the service area to pick up four plates of chow mein.

'Jake?' she says. 'Any chance you can lend a hand out front for a minute? Mr Zhao is taking a phone call from the wholesaler and table six needs to be cleared.'

'I'm on it,' I say, straightening my apron and picking up a tray.

Table six is the central, circular table Mum was serving when I first arrived. The businessmen and women are chilled and mellow and happy now, chatting easily and sipping jasmine tea or glasses of wine. I put down my tray and begin to clear the dishes away, polite and smiling, but a little nervous.

Mr Zhao doesn't like me to be out front too much. I am

too young, too clueless, not smart enough. If I do need to help out, he prefers me to be invisible. I can see him at the back of the restaurant, chatting on his mobile, his eagle eyes watching me as I gather up the used napkins.

As I lean across to rescue an abandoned teaspoon, a drop of liquid plops on to the tablecloth. I frown, pick up a napkin and dab it away, but as I reach over another drop of water lands right in front of me.

'What's that, mate?' one of the businessmen asks.

'I don't know . . .'

A third drop of water lands in the centre of the table, and in unison we all look upwards to where the drips are coming from.

The ceiling above us is stained dark, bulging down towards us horribly. It looks all wrong, terrifying somehow, like the time I broke my wrist when I was eight and one of the bones poked out under the skin in a very alarming way. As we watch, the ceiling seems to shudder. It quivers, and there's a collective intake of breath from those gathered round the table.

'Doesn't look right, that,' one of the men comments, which may well be the understatement of the year.

❀❀❀❀❀❀❀❀❀❀❀❀❀❀❀❀❀❀❀❀❀❀❀

And then the bulging ceiling collapses, and a torrent of lukewarm water gushes down on to the table, drenching the diners, drenching me, smashing and soaking everything. People are screaming and swearing and yelling, leaping up, jumping back, asking what the heck is going on. The table is covered with soaked and splintered wood, mushy plaster and flakes of paint, scattered artfully among the knives and forks and overturned teacups. And then, as quickly as it began, the waterfall slows to a dribble.

I can see Mr Zhao at the back of the restaurant, his mouth agape, the mobile phone dropping from his hand. I can see Mum, frozen in time, her face a mask of horror as she surveys the carnage.

The last thing to fall from the gaping hole in the ceiling is a pair of waterlogged jeans, complete with a very faint soy-sauce stain on one leg.

Kill me now.

3

A silence falls, heavy and ominous, and after the silence comes uproar. Mr Zhao loses it big style. His face is a kind of mottled purple and his voice is like the bellow of an angry bull.

'What have you done?' he roars. 'What. Have. You. *Done*?'

I am not sure that he actually requires an answer, but staying silent has never been my strong point.

'I was washing stuff in the bath,' I say, picking up the soaking jeans and trying for a smile. 'There was a soy-sauce stain on my Levis –'

'Washing stuff in the bath?' Mr Zhao echoes. 'The *bath*? What's wrong with a washing machine, or the sink? What's wrong with switching the taps off? What's wrong with *you*, Jake Cooke?'

There are quite a few things wrong with me according to my school teachers, an inability to keep my mouth shut being one of them, but in the heat of the moment I somehow forget this.

'Chill,' I say brightly. 'Look at it this way, you won't have to mop the floor for a while.'

I can see Mum covering her face with one hand, distraught. I know that look. I've seen it too many times, and too late I realize that my cheap joke has made things worse.

'You think this is *funny*?' Mr Zhao bellows. 'Your stupid trick has destroyed my restaurant, my livelihood – and you think it's one big *joke*? Get out of my sight before I do something I'll regret!'

I take a step backwards, my trainers squelching as I go, but the customers block my escape, and they're angry now as well.

'How can it be the kid's fault?' one dripping diner demands. 'Your ceiling just fell down! I've got a good mind to call the environmental health.'

'I'll be sending you a bill for my jacket,' another tells Mr Zhao. 'This is disgraceful!'

Mr Zhao switches tone. 'I'm so, so sorry,' he pleads, trying to usher the drenched customers out. 'I can assure you I will personally honour any dry-cleaning bills, and I am deeply sorry for the inconvenience. Your next meal is free, of course, on the house. Please do come back . . .'

But the customers are leaving, not just those who got wet but the others too, shaking their heads and pursing their lips, abandoning their food to take sneaky photos of the chaos with their mobiles.

Mum appears at my shoulder, white with shock. 'Mr Zhao, listen –' she begins, but our boss is way too angry for that.

'Listen?' he snarls. '*Listen?* No, *you* will listen to me, Alison Cooke. I should have known you were trouble the moment I set eyes on you – you and those good-for-nothing kids of yours. You've ruined me; ruined me! Get out of my sight!'

I lie awake all night on the top bunk, running through everything in my head until I think it will drive me mad. Why didn't I take the plug out, empty the bath before I left? Why didn't I wait for Gran, call down and say I'd be late for my shift? Why did I even care about those stupid jeans in the first place?

Last night Harry texted to call off our big night out anyway – his brother told him that the venue has a very strict over-18s admission code, and no amount of fake ID would convince them that the three of us are that old. So, yeah, all for nothing.

It turns out that Maisie and Isla had decided to tidy up the bathroom before Gran arrived. Maisie was rinsing my jeans when a pound coin dropped out of the pocket; the two of them dived for it, rescued it and abandoned the bath and the still-running taps to run down to the corner shop for a packet of Jammie Dodgers. On the way back they bumped into Gran, who took them to the park for a go on the swings. The three of them arrived back at the flat roughly ten minutes after the floor caved in. Sweet.

See, whichever way you look at it, it was my fault. I filled the bath and assumed that a heap of soapy bubbles and a *Frozen* DVD would do instead of a babysitter, even though I knew Gran was delayed. I even, somehow, left a pound coin in my jeans pocket; that was what sealed my fate.

Maybe Maisie was the one who switched the taps on,

but she was only trying to help. I shouldn't have left her in charge of Isla, especially not beside a bathtub full of water.

I fall asleep sometime after 5 a.m. and end up sleeping in; by the time I surface again, it's almost midday and I can hear voices in the living room.

I creep to the door and press my ear against it, and there is the sound of my little sisters bickering gently in front of the TV and the much more alarming sound of Mum arguing with Mr Zhao.

'You must not use the bathroom,' he is saying. 'No, no, no. I have covered the hole in the floor with a sheet of hardboard, but I cannot take responsibility for how safe it is. Keep the kids out of there. It's a pity you didn't do that yesterday!'

'Mr Zhao, we have apologized over and over,' Mum replies. 'What more do you want, blood? And how do you expect me to keep the kids out of the bathroom? We have to wash!'

Mr Zhao mutters something about this not being a problem we'll have to put up with for much longer, and I groan. It doesn't sound as if he has forgiven us yet for yesterday's bathroom tsunami. He mentions something about the restaurant being closed until the repairs can be made, about how it could be wise to move out sooner rather than later.

A cold wave of panic washes over me. Moving out? What does he mean?

I press my ear to the door again.

'Let's face it,' Mr Zhao is saying. 'This flat is in no fit state for anyone to live in. It's a disaster zone; a health hazard!'

I grit my teeth. The flat may be a disaster zone, but it's also our home. Though probably not for much longer.

'Give me a little bit of time,' Mum is saying. 'I'll need to talk to the kids, explain what's happening and we'll need a few days to pack.'

I peer through the crack in the door and see Mr Zhao standing with his arms folded, his face like stone. This is his usual look, to be fair.

'Of course, of course,' Mr Zhao says gruffly. 'It's not as though I will be throwing you out on the streets, is it?'

'We'll move out a week on Saturday,' Mum says, her shoulders drooping. 'I'm sorry that it had to end like this.'

'Me too,' Mr Zhao says. 'Me too, Alison Cooke.'

I bite down on my sleeve to stop myself from yelling

✿✿✿✿✿✿✿✿✿✿✿✿✿✿✿✿✿✿✿✿✿✿✿

abuse at our ex-landlord; I guess I have landed us all in enough trouble already. I didn't think that things could actually get any worse, but, as usual, I was wrong.

It looks like we are being evicted.

It's an all-time low, even for me.

4

Mr Zhao has draped orange hazard tape all round the bathroom; the place looks like some kind of crime scene. Which it probably is, from Mr Zhao's point of view. I manage a makeshift wash at the sink, pull on yesterday's trackies and a T-shirt and pad though to the living room. The carpet squelches beneath my bare feet as I drift across to the kitchenette and pour cornflakes and milk into a bowl.

Mum has the heating on full blast, so the place feels like a sauna; all the windows are open and my little sisters are watching kids' TV in their bikinis.

Mum makes herself a mug of tea; she looks tired, frayed around the edges.

'So,' I say, trying for a chirpy tone. 'When do we move?'

Mum sighs. 'You were listening? I was going to tell you,

Jake. In my own time. Can we keep this quiet for a little while, for the sake of the girls?'

My eyes slide over to my little sisters, who have abandoned the TV now to act out some kind of flood disaster game with the broken Barbie dolls. It makes my gut twist to know that my carelessness has wrecked everything for them.

'What will happen?' I ask quietly. 'Will we squash in with Gran for a while? Look for a new flat? Or find some scaffy B&B?'

Mum rolls her eyes. 'None of those things, Jake,' she says, and casually drops a bombshell even bigger than the great bathtub tsumani. 'You see, I've met a man. A very nice man, a kind man – someone I'd like to be a part of my life. Our lives. So this seems like fate, in a way. We'll be moving in with him.'

I just about choke on my cornflakes.

Mum flicks on her smartphone and shows me pictures of the new boyfriend; he is thin and tanned and beardy, with long dreadlocks tied back in a ponytail and a T-shirt that says Free Tibet. I always thought Tibet was a country, not some kind of supermarket special deal.

I cringe at the very sight of him.

'No way,' I say. 'Mum, he's a full-on weirdo!'

'He's no such thing,' Mum insists. 'He's gentle and kind and open-minded enough to take on a new relationship with a single mother of three. That's quite something.'

I look across the living room to where Isla and Maisie are digging up a wilting potted plant to bury a Barbie doll. The beardy guy has no clue what he is signing up for.

'He's Lou Parker's brother's friend,' Mum goes on, naming an old friend of hers with pink dip-dyed hair and multiply pierced ears. 'I met him at one of her parties years ago. Then last month when I went on that weekend reflexology course, he was there too, teaching t'ai chi. It was just like we were fated to meet again!'

It's not fate as far as I am concerned, more of a sick joke, but I keep my mouth shut. Mum is a great believer in fate, along with fortune cookies, horoscopes, yoga and herbal remedies. When I got nits back in Year Four she slathered my head with so much tea tree oil I smelled like Vicks VapoRub for months, and nobody would sit near me in class. No wonder the nits kept away.

'Who is this creep?' I ask. 'What's his name?'

Mum shakes her head. 'He's not a creep, Jake! He's called Pete Shedden, but everybody calls him Sheddie. He's great; you'll like him.'

'Sheddie?' I echo. 'Sheddie! Seriously? That's not a real name!'

'It's a nickname,' Mum repeats patiently. 'I told you. Just give this a chance!'

I don't want to give any chances at all to a weedy beardy guy who seems to be named after a garden hut. A chance like that could mess with everything. In all of my life, I can't remember staying anywhere for more than a couple of years. Even when Mum was with Rick, we moved all the time because he was never able to hold down a job for long.

Past homes I have known: Gran's house in Bethnal Green, when I was really little; a bedsit two streets from Gran's when she and Mum fell out; a bunch of different flats and terraced houses when we lived with Rick in Manchester; and now a poky flat over a restaurant in Chinatown.

I do not want to pack up and start from scratch again, playing happy families with some long-haired crusty with

· 33

the worst nickname in the world. This has disaster written all over it.

My sisters appear, distracted at last from their Barbie burial by the sound of raised voices and the fizz of panic in the air. They crowd on to the sofa, pressing themselves close to Mum, eyeing me anxiously.

'Are we moving?' Isla wants to know.

'Well, the flat's not at its best right now,' Mum says, trying to be bright and breezy. 'So, yes, I think it could be a good time to move. We'll be heading for the Midlands, a town called Millford. There's a big rambling house on the edge of a park, with a garden and everything!'

A wave of hurt and anger rolls through me. She has it all planned out; we get no say at all.

'Will we have our own rooms?' Maisie asks.

Mum frowns. 'I'm not exactly sure if we'll be in the house, to begin with anyway.'

My eyes open wide. 'Not in the house?' I repeat. 'Huh? Where else would we be? In a tent in the garden?'

Mum looks awkward. 'It's a yurt, actually,' she says, and I start to laugh because I cannot believe my mum can even think about dragging us halfway across the country to live in a yurt in some miserable north-of-nowhere dump. Then I remember that we are being evicted, and that it's all my fault and I stop laughing.

'Is it a holiday?' Isla is asking. 'Because if it is, I would rather go to the Costa del Sol. Evie Flucker went there at half-term and they stayed in a big hotel with a swimming pool. She got this cool stuffed donkey wearing a sunhat as a souvenir. I think that might be better than camping –'

'It's not a holiday,' Maisie cuts in. 'It's forever, isn't it, Mum? It might actually be the perfect time to get a dog. A labradoodle? Because they are very cute, and I have always wanted a pet.'

'We'll see,' Mum says. 'I think there are chickens, and Sheddie grows his own vegetables so we will be practically self-sufficient.'

'Chickens?' Maisie echoes.

'Vegetables?' Isla chimes in.

You have to remember that they have spent the last two years living above The Paper Dragon. Their idea of home-grown food is sweet and sour pork and egg-fried rice eaten lukewarm out of silver foil boxes.

Isla frowns. 'Who is *Sheddie*?' she asks.

❀❀❀❀❀❀❀❀❀❀❀❀❀❀❀❀❀❀❀❀

Mum actually blushes and starts explaining that Sheddie is a nice man, a t'ai chi instructor and youth worker who makes willow sculptures in his spare time.

'Yes, but who *is* he?' my littlest sister presses. 'Is he your boyfriend?'

'I suppose he is,' Mum admits. 'You'll like him, Isla. You all will! He is coming to stay for a few days, so you can get to know him, and then we can all go to Millford together!'

This isn't just a whirlwind romance; it's practically a tornado. Mum is thinking on her feet, making the best of a disastrous situation, but there's no way on earth she'd be considering a move like this if we weren't being evicted. And I for one do not want to be pulled from the wreckage of yesterday's flood by a dreadlocked crusty called Sheddie. It feels dodgy, dangerous; like jumping from the frying pan into the fire.

'And we're moving a week on Saturday?' I check.

'It'll give us time to pack,' Mum says. 'This is all for the best, Jake; please try to understand!'

But I don't understand anything, except that life is turning upside down again, and somehow it's all my fault. Anger boils up inside me, a bubbling soup of fury; I have messed up yet again and this time, finally, I have ruined everything. We're evicted, homeless; doomed to live in a scabby tent with some hopeless hippy – and who do I have to blame for it all? Me, me, me.

I'm on my feet, swearing under my breath as I storm out of the room, slamming the door so hard it almost comes off its hinges. Literally. I don't even care – the rest of the flat is falling to bits, so what does a bit more damage matter? A few flakes of plaster flutter down around my head like fake snowflakes as I climb up the ladder to the top bunk, the only place I can get any privacy in this stupid place. If I think this is bad, what will a yurt be like?

I fling myself down on the mattress, blinking back angry tears; I won't cry, I won't. Instead, I clench my hands so hard the fingernails dig into my palms, drawing blood. How come some people are so unlucky? It's the story of my life. At school, Harry and Mitch are the troublemakers, the stirrers, but I'm the one who lands myself in trouble, over and over again. I'm either in the wrong place at the wrong time, or I can't resist the temptation to open my mouth and say something smart. Neither trait is anything to be proud of.

My flaws have caught up with me big style, and my mum

and sisters are paying the price for them this time, not just me. If only I had a wad of money to help fix the damage I've caused; I bet Mr Zhao wouldn't be turfing us out then. The guilt curdles into anger again, a toxic, choking anger that makes me want to yell and roar and break things. I slam one fist against the wall, making the whole bunk – the whole wall – shake.

No plaster falls down on my head this time, but a couple of drawing pins come loose and the train ticket to Somerset and the fortune cookie prediction from our first day in Chinatown drift down softly on to the faded duvet.

Soon life will become more interesting, it says.

It seems like a sign.

5

So, yeah. This is how I come to be walking the streets of London at 4 a.m. in the morning, carrying a rucksack and the weight of the world on my shoulders. I am fourteen years old and I have a train ticket to Somerset and a letter from a mad girl who says she is my half-sister. I also have a gutful of guilt and plenty of determination to fix things, sort things, put things right. I just haven't worked out how. Not yet, not exactly; but I will. I have the start of an idea.

I am wearing the soy-sauce jeans and I've packed cheese sandwiches, a packet of crisps, spare socks, a change of T-shirt. In my pocket the train ticket and the fortune cookie prediction sit alongside the princely sum of £9.52, which is my entire life savings.

It's time to take a risk of my own.

It's a Saturday, but the tubes aren't running yet, so I walk towards the nearest overground station. I pass homeless people sleeping in doorways, in sleeping bags beneath polythene sheets. My heart thumps; I need to find a solution to this mess, and fast, or it could be us out on the streets.

It turns out that trains to Exeter don't leave from Charing Cross; I need to go to Waterloo, so I head on over the bridge, the Thames glinting pink and gold as I pass above it. Once there, I discover that my ticket isn't valid until after nine, so I buy a hot chocolate from a mobile coffee stall that's just opening up, then sit for a while and work on my plan.

I am running away from the mess I've made, leaving behind the chaos of life as I know it. It sounds like a coward's way out, but it isn't really. I will give myself a week to find an answer, to save my family from eviction and disaster. I am not a runaway; I'm on a mission.

The message I scrawled on the window of The Paper Dragon before I left was an apology to Mr Zhao. I don't think it's fair that Mum, Isla and Maisie should be punished for my mistake, and with me out of the picture maybe

✿✿✿✿✿✿✿✿✿✿✿✿✿✿✿✿✿✿✿✿✿

things can settle down again, go back to normal. Maybe Mum won't feel like she has to hook up with that creep Sheddie to get us out of trouble.

I am not stupid; I know my apology won't undo the damage, but I have a plan for that too. It's a mad plan, and it might not work, but it has to be worth a try.

I am going to find my dad. It's not because I have a dad-shaped hole in my life, or because I need to meet him, shake him by the hand, bond with him and hear his side of the story. It's not even so I can tell him I'm doing fine without him.

It's way more mercenary than that; I want his money.

The way I see it, my dad owes me – big time. He hasn't been around to see me grow up; not one visit, not one card, not even a phone call to check in from time to time. I could be sick in hospital with some life-threatening disease and he wouldn't know; I could be a juvenile delinquent, a criminal in the making. Actually, scrap that, it's a little too close to the truth.

What I'm saying is: he has never given me anything, not one thing, my whole entire life. I know Mum doesn't get maintenance money; if she did, it would have kept us out of poverty, kept Mum from working the night shift at the supermarket in Manchester, stopped her working a seven-day week at The Paper Dragon. If my dad had put his hand in his pocket and coughed up some maintenance, we'd have had the money to repair the broken washing machine or the cash for a launderette wash. I wouldn't have had to kneel on the floor washing my favourite jeans in the bath. And while I'm being honest, let's be clear on this; when I say 'favourite', I mean 'only'.

I am not under any illusion that my dad is a great bloke. I think he's a loser, but from what Honey says he is a loser with money.

I have never taken a thing from him, but now I need his help. I want him to pay for the repairs to the ceiling at The Paper Dragon and the bathroom floor in the flat. This would rescue Mr Zhao from certain ruin, maybe save us from eviction. It might save us from a grim future as yurt-dwelling hippies too – surely my dad would help us find a decent flat, one where there's no mould on the walls.

If I'm lucky, my new half-sisters will help me make contact with him, help me to appeal to him for help. It's a half-baked plan, but it's better than no plan at all.

❀❀❀❀❀❀❀❀❀❀❀❀❀❀❀❀❀❀❀❀❀

In the meantime, I have somewhere to lie low for a while and get to know my new sisters. I admit it, I'm curious. Four half-sisters who share my DNA, my colouring, my looks; what else might they share? Will they understand me, like me, see a potential in me instead of just a talent for wrecking everything I touch?

I can hope, I guess.

Finally, I make it on to a train, and soon I am speeding out of London, eating cheese sandwiches to celebrate my escape from angry landlords, t'ai chi and dreadlocks.

It's kind of exhilarating.

I take out my mobile and text Maisie. I saved my Paper Dragon wages from the Easter holidays to buy my cheapo pay-as-you-go mobile, and Maisie's phone is an ancient hand-me-down from Gran, only to be used in emergencies. This feels like an emergency to me.

You OK? I ask. **Don't show anyone this text. Let me know when you're alone and I'll try to call you.**

Minutes later, a reply bleeps through.

Can you call now? Please? I've locked myself in the bathroom with the taps running.

I press CALL in a panic, and seconds later the call connects.

'Why are the taps running?' I demand. 'What's going on? Be careful, Maisie!'

'So Mum thinks I'm washing, of course,' she hisses. 'I'm not going to flood anything. D'you think I'm stupid?'

'No!' I tell her. 'Just checking. So, nobody can hear you? Are you sure?'

'I'm sure,' she promises. 'Mum's hoovering and Isla is watching CBeebies.'

'OK. Don't tell anyone I've called,' I say. 'Don't mention that you saw me leaving. Promise, Maisie? It's really, really important.'

'I promise,' she says in a small voice. 'I won't. But – oh, Cookie, have you run away for ever and ever?'

'No way!' I tell her. 'I'm going to fix everything, OK? For Mr Zhao, for Mum, for all of us. We won't have to go and live in a tent with Mum's stupid hippy boyfriend. We can stay where we are, only the flat will be all sorted and nice and the restaurant will be good as new. Or maybe we'll have a new flat, with a bedroom each. I'm working on it. I'll be back as soon as I can, and meanwhile, Maisie, you have to cover for me if you can. OK?'

'I already am, Cookie,' she says. 'Mr Zhao just hammered

on our door to tell Mum you wrote graffiti all over the restaurant window. Mum is not happy. She said something about her new red lipstick.'

'I thought they'd be pleased I didn't use spray paint,' I say with a sigh. 'I wanted him to know I was sorry, that's all!'

'I think the whole street knows you're sorry,' Maisie says. 'Anyhow, Mum is angry too now; she says you've put your foot in it again. She came raging into the bedroom looking for you, but I said you'd gone over to Harry's.'

'Thanks, Maisie,' I say. 'Good save.'

'Will you be back later?' my little sister asks, plaintive now. 'Please come back. That horrible hippy man is coming to visit tomorrow, and Mum keeps talking about the yurt-thing.'

Maisie's words are starting to break up as the train gathers speed.

'Listen; I won't be back today, Maisie,' I reply, trying to talk slowly and clearly. 'I might be a bit longer than that, but don't worry about the hippy guy or the yurt-thing. I'll sort all that, OK? Just promise not to tell and keep covering for me, OK? And, Maisie, switch those taps off!'

45

❀❀❀❀❀❀❀❀❀❀❀❀❀❀❀❀❀❀❀❀

I finally lose signal completely; my mobile goes dead, and I just have to hope she's got the message. I sigh. Even my scrawled apology has been dismissed as graffiti; I can't get anything right. Still, at least Maisie hasn't blabbed; she's actually put Mum off the scent with her story that I've gone over to Harry's. Mum's clearly not pleased, but she's probably not surprised either. She'll assume I'm staying out of the way for Sheddie's arrival, hiding out at Harry's for a bit. That's probably what I would have done, if it weren't for this magic ticket.

Once I get a mobile signal again, I ping off a couple of texts to Harry and Mitch to explain what's going on and ask them to say the right things if Mum happens to call them. Next I text Mum, a brief message telling her I'm staying at Harry's for a couple of days until Mr Zhao cools down. **Don't worry**, I type. **I will be back by the end of the week, and maybe things will be looking better by then. Sorry for being such a disaster zone. Love Jake x**

I put away my mobile and stare out of the train window and allow myself to hope that things will work out.

Fate is all well and good, but it doesn't mean sitting

around on the sidelines while life lurches from bad to worse. You can take control, steer things in a different direction, make a stand when everyone around you is hell-bent on disaster.

It beats feeling angry and helpless anyhow.

I am not running away so much as embarking on an adventure to put right some of the world's wrongs. I am a teenage superhero in slightly stained jeans and a faded T-shirt, seeking justice for all – plus a new ceiling and a patched-up bathroom floor.

It doesn't seem like too much to ask.

6

It takes ages to get to Exeter, and once I'm there it turns out that I still have miles and miles to travel; I have to take not one but *two* buses onwards. I manage to get away without paying the fares by sneaking on to the first bus with a student group and then with a family of tourists on the second, but still, I am starting to lose the will to live. Who knows, maybe life in a no-hope Midlands town would be better than life in the wilds of Somerset, because all I can see from the bus window is mile after mile of moorland with the occasional desolate village scattered about just to relieve the boredom. Except that it doesn't, not quite.

No wonder my mysterious half-sister Honey decided to track me down – life out in the sticks must be painfully dull.

Finally, I get off the bus in Kitnor and ask directions to Tanglewood from a woman in the high street.

She scribbles a makeshift map on the back of an old envelope and I thank her and trudge up the lane towards Tanglewood wondering if this whole trip is a mistake. What if the letters are the ravings of a deranged mind, or a sick practical joke? Then I remember the photo of the blonde-haired sisters who look so like me, and I know that's not so.

This is an adventure, a quest to find my long-lost family, find out the truth about my no-good dad and put a few things right again. It's a chance to rescue my family from certain doom, and I only have seven days to manage it. I will not chicken out.

I won't lie, though. I am shaking in my shoes as I walk across the gravel driveway towards the big Victorian house. The place looks busy – there are no fewer than five cars and two fancy-looking vans parked outside, and I can see a whole bunch of people through the window near what looks like the back door.

Some kind of party must be going on.

I walk up to the door, take a deep breath and knock three times.

The door is opened by a spectacled young man carrying one of those outsize microphones you sometimes see on TV; it's kind of fluffy and a little bit intimidating.

I glance at the map on the back of the envelope again, frowning. This doesn't feel quite right, but I know I haven't made any wrong turnings, and besides, there was a sign saying Tanglewood on the gatepost.

What is going on?

'Oh, it's you!' the young man says, as if he's been expecting me. 'You're an hour early. Where's the guitar?'

'No idea,' I say. 'What guitar?'

'Funny,' he says, deadpan. 'Any chance you can nip home and fetch it?'

'No chance at all,' I reply.

I have no idea who this man thinks I am, but there is no point pretending. I do not own a guitar. I do not own a kazoo, come to that. I don't have a musical bone in my body.

'For goodness' sake,' the man grumbles. 'I just do not understand kids today. This is TV. This could be your big

❀❀❀❀❀❀❀❀❀❀❀❀❀❀❀❀❀❀❀❀

break, kid, and you're just not bothered. Come in, anyway. You can help with the packing boxes scene. Get on with it. Act natural.'

Act natural? Get on with it? I resist the impulse to turn round and walk away and step into the crowded kitchen, trying to look as casual as I can.

It's like stepping into insanity.

I am not kidding; this kitchen has an entire film crew in it. The room is stuffed with cameras, mics, booms and huge super-bright spotlights. Giant white and silver umbrellas jostle for space, reflecting light everywhere; people are adjusting cameras, zooming in, positioning mics.

And all this paraphernalia is pointed at the kitchen table, where a family is sitting, packing bright, beribboned chocolate boxes into a big crate. I spot my stalker, prettier than her photograph, looking bored and irritable; two girls who must be the twins, the dark-haired stepsister and the youngest one, pulling an outraged face as her cheeks are dusted with powder by a woman who seems to be a make-up artist.

A fair-haired woman and a dark-haired man are standing behind the table, watching the film crew as if waiting for instructions.

Bizarre.

The good thing is, I seem to be invisible. Let's face it, there are so many people in this room that one more isn't really going to make a difference.

'OK, we'll take that from the top,' a woman with a clipboard says with authority, and the chat fizzles out at once. 'Paddy, Charlotte, I want you to tell the girls about your new order and ask them to help you pack up the chocolates. OK?'

'OK,' everybody says.

'And go,' the clipboard woman says. 'Right. We are rolling. Everybody act natural; we'll shoot it all and edit afterwards, so don't worry if you make a mistake. Pretend we're not here. We want natural, unguarded, fly-on-the-wall type coverage. Go!'

'What about the boy?' the mic guy who let me in asks. 'D'you want him at the table too?'

'What boy?' the clipboard woman asks, frowning.

The mic guy turns to look at me. 'The kid with the guitar,' he says. 'Only he's forgotten to bring it. What did you say your name was?'

'I didn't,' I say brightly.

All eyes turn to me, accusing. Whoever Guitar Boy is, they know I am not him.

'I don't think we know you, do we?' the dark-haired man asks politely.

I smile nervously. 'No, I don't think you do . . .'

The fair-haired woman, her arms full of brightly-wrapped chocolate boxes, tilts her head to one side. 'So, you are?'

I open my mouth and close it again, at a loss.

Too late, I remember a snippet from one of the letters.

'I still haven't told them about you, but they're going to be so amazed . . .'

She still hasn't told them.

I have made a terrible mistake; what was I even thinking? It seemed so simple in my head, just a case of turning up and asking for my dad's contact details, then collecting a wodge of cash to sort out all our troubles. I should have known it wouldn't be that easy. With me, nothing ever is.

I'm still struggling to get to grips with the idea that my new half-sisters exist, but apart from Honey, my letter-writing stalker, they have absolutely no idea about me; none at all. And trying to explain things in the middle of a crowded kitchen with a film crew recording every moment; well, let's just say it's not ideal.

I look at the faces of my half-sisters, sitting round the table. Blank. Frowning. Confused. Until I get to Honey, that is. Her eyes are wide, her mouth a perfect 'o' of surprise.

'Jake?' she whispers. 'Is it you? Really?'

I throw my rail ticket down on the table, trying for a smile.

'I was just passing, so I thought I'd drop in. But I can see you're kind of busy . . .'

I take a step back and bump into the sink. My exit is blocked by the film crew, and when Honey gets to her feet and sprints across the kitchen towards me there is literally no escape.

'Oh. My. God!' she shrieks. 'Jake! It's you! It's really *you*!'

She throws her arms round me and hugs me tight, and I panic slightly, especially when one of the cameras zooms in close to record the moment. I wonder if it is capturing the look of terror on my face as Honey finally releases me and holds me at arm's length.

'Who's Jake?' the youngest half-sister asks. 'I don't get it!'

'Nobody gets it,' another sister chips in. 'Honey, are you going to explain? Who's your friend?'

'Yes, Honey, what's going on?' the fair-haired woman wants to know.

She turns to face her family.

'You're never going to believe it,' Honey says. 'This is Jake Cooke, and I found out about him while I was living with Dad in Sydney. He's fourteen – so a little bit older than Coco and younger than the twins. Does the name mean anything to you, Mum? Jake Cooke?'

'Not a thing,' the woman whispers, but there's a tremor in her voice and I can feel her looking at me hard, like I am some kind of puzzle she is trying to work out. Her eyes narrow and her eyebrows slant upwards in surprise, and I can only imagine the thoughts that are going on behind those expressions.

'I wasn't supposed to find out,' Honey is saying. 'I wasn't meant to, obviously, but I did, and I thought I'd write and make contact with him before I told you all. And now he's here, and I never did get around to explaining, because . . . well, because I wasn't sure what to say. How to break the news. I didn't want to upset you, Mum.

And I had no idea that Jake would just turn up out of the blue . . .'

I find myself eyeing the rail ticket on the table. I am beginning to wish I had never seen it.

Honey grabs me by the elbows and propels me forward.

'Look, this is going to come as a shock. There's no easy way to say it. So – oh, Jake, just tell them who you are!'

My throat feels dry as dust; speech seems impossible. One of those furry mics appears, hovering just above my head, dangling from an extendable stick.

Honey prods me forward again. 'Go on!' she hisses. 'Just say it!'

So I do.

'I'm Jake, and I think I am Honey's half-brother,' I croak out. I scan the faces at the table, watching me now with a mixture of astonishment and horror. 'So, yeah, probably your half-brother too. Small world, huh?'

Honey steps forward to stand beside me.

'Dad had an affair,' she says in a small voice. 'Years ago, when we were tiny. Jake was the result. I found out about it and I wrote to Jake, and, well – here he is. I mean, he's family, right?'

❀❀❀❀❀❀❀❀❀❀❀❀❀❀❀❀❀❀❀❀❀❀❀

The fair-haired woman, clearly Honey's mum, drops the armful of chocolate boxes she is holding and slumps down on to a kitchen chair, her face bleached white.

'Cut!' the woman with the clipboard says into the silence. 'Cut, everybody. Cut. So, can anybody tell me what just happened?'

Nobody says a thing, and the guy with the spectacles and the fluffy mic raises an eyebrow, smiling.

'Well,' he says. 'I'm not sure, but I think we just recorded ourselves some pure TV gold . . .'

7

Everything is chaos after that. The half-sisters are all talking at once, loudly and angrily; the fair-haired woman, Charlotte, who is clearly the girls' mum, is crying; and the dark-haired man with the blue twinkly eyes is shaking his head and asking the film crew if everyone can have a bit of a break.

'We need some time out here to talk,' he is saying. 'This is family stuff, not TV stuff. OK?'

'No worries, Paddy,' the clipboard woman says reassuringly. 'We'll wrap for today, give you some space. Let's start over in the morning – ten-ish?'

'Sure,' the twinkly guy says. 'Fine.'

'I should go too,' I mutter, but Honey grabs my arm and anchors me still.

'Don't you dare,' she says. 'It took long enough to find you and get you here; you can't run away now!'

'She's right,' Paddy says. 'We need to talk. Let's leave the TV crew to pack up. C'mon, we'll head through to the living room; get a bit of peace and quiet.'

He herds everyone out of the kitchen, away from the bustle of cameras and mics being packed away, the dismantling of lights and reflectors. I am ushered through a wide hallway lined with framed paintings that look like they were done by my half-sisters at an early age: all spattered paint and spindly stick figures and huge amounts of glitter. I feel a strange twist of emotion at seeing them: happy for the half-sisters, sad for me. I remember a couple of my hand-made Christmas cards being propped on a window sill at our old bedsit in London, in pre-Rick times, and an especially lurid collage involving pasta shapes that Isla once made Sellotaped to the fridge for a while when we lived in Manchester. Kids' artwork framed and hung on the walls, though? It's a whole different world.

And then I'm in the living room, and that's a whole different world too; there are blue velvet sofas and an open fire with Victorian tiles and a carved wooden fire surround,

❀❀❀❀❀❀❀❀❀❀❀❀❀❀❀❀❀❀❀❀❀

a big pile of floor cushions and a blue oriental-looking rug that's threadbare in a couple of places and is most likely worth a small fortune. The sisters flop down on the sofas, still chattering and whispering, Charlotte sinks into a drooping armchair, and Paddy indicates that I should sit down too. I pull a couple of floor cushions next to the fire and sit down warily, poised for flight.

'The TV crew are gone,' Paddy says, peering out through the window; I glimpse a flash of slow-moving vehicles crunching across the gravel. 'Thank goodness. That was spectacularly bad timing. I think they got a bit more than they bargained for today!'

'We don't always have cameras and lights in the kitchen,' the youngest sister pipes up, throwing me an uncertain smile. 'They're filming a reality TV series based on us, and the chocolate business . . .'

'I don't think I mentioned the chocolate business,' Honey frowns. 'Mum and Paddy make luxury fair-trade truffles: The Chocolate Box. You might have heard of it?'

I blink and shrug helplessly.

I have been known to scarf down a bar of Cadbury's

❀❀❀❀❀❀❀❀❀❀❀❀❀❀❀❀❀❀❀❀❀

Fruit and Nut or a Snickers bar, but luxury fair-trade truffles? I wouldn't know one if it fell from the skies right into my mouth.

'Will they actually use that clip of film, do you think?' Charlotte asks in a whisper. 'I mean, I'm sure it's all very entertaining, but I am not sure I want Greg's little secret broadcast to the nation.'

My cheeks sting with colour. So I am not a brand-new half-brother, I am Greg's 'little secret', something to be hidden away, hushed up, covered up. I must have been crazy to imagine I might be welcome here.

'I'll talk to them, don't worry,' Paddy says. 'There are all kinds of privacy issues involved. I don't suppose Jake knew quite what he was walking into.'

'You definitely picked your moment,' Honey says to me. 'Lights, camera, action: cue the long-lost brother!'

'I wasn't exactly lost,' I mutter.

'No, but you're a bit of a surprise, all the same,' Charlotte says. 'I wish you'd told me, Honey. Meeting Jake like this out of the blue – well, it's a massive shock to the system. I can't seem to take it in!'

Honey pouts. 'I wanted to tell you,' she says. 'It was just

hard to find the words. I'm really sorry, Mum! I didn't mean to upset you!'

Charlotte blots her eyes with a tissue, squaring her shoulders. I cannot tell what she's thinking, but I am willing to bet it's not exactly friendly.

'So,' she says. 'You are Jake Cooke?'

'That's right,' I say, squirming a little and resisting the temptation to make a mock salute. 'Jake Cooke, that's me. Sorry to show up unannounced. I didn't really have time to plan it. I'd have called if I'd had a contact number, probably. Or maybe I shouldn't have come at all; it was a really, really bad idea.'

The woman pushes her hair back, struggles to smile.

'No, no, of course it wasn't,' she says, shaking her head softly. 'It was exactly the right thing to do. I mean, I can't pretend this isn't difficult – painful, even – but you are welcome, Jake. I mean that. If we are not being too hospitable, well, I think it's just that we're struggling a little to absorb it all.'

That opens the floodgates.

'You're our half-brother?' the littlest half-sister marvels. 'And nobody ever knew? So what's the story?'

62

'I can't take it in,' one of the twins says. 'We were tiny babies and Coco wasn't even born yet, and Dad didn't care at all; he turned his back on us all to go off with your mum! It's like everything I ever believed was a lie.'

'Was Dad actually living with you and your mum?' the other twin demands. 'While he was still with us? Like some kind of double life?'

I don't know how to even start to answer.

'I never met him,' I offer, as if that might make my new half-sisters a fraction less hostile. 'He left my mum before I was born. I only found out who he was when Honey wrote. Mum met him when she was eighteen or nineteen; they worked in the same place, I think. I'm not sure she even knew he was married . . .'

'Eighteen or nineteen,' Charlotte echoes. 'So she wasn't much more than a child herself; and I had no idea. No idea at all.'

She smiles and shakes her head, but her eyes brim with tears again and I feel like the worst person in the world. Maybe I take after my no-good dad? I probably do. Half my genes come from him, after all. It could explain a lot.

'Turns out Dad was a loser all along,' Honey says. 'He

was just generally useless at being a husband and a dad. Sorry, Mum, but he was! It took me long enough to see it, but it wasn't your fault; it wasn't anybody's. Dad's kind of hopeless. It's not like he's even improved or learnt from his mistakes; he's pretty rubbish.'

'He is,' Charlotte agrees. 'And it hurts to be reminded of it all, but,well, we've moved on, haven't we? We're a better, happier family now. And if we hadn't been through all that I'd never be with Paddy now, and he is my absolute soulmate; I can't imagine this family without him.'

Honey rolls her eyes and shakes her head, but I notice the flicker of a grin tugging at the corner of her mouth. I'd guess her relationship with Paddy hasn't always run smoothly. Maybe I will tell her about Sheddie and his yurt sometime; she'll realize just how lucky she is.

I am kind of impressed at how Charlotte has soaked up the bombshell and recovered so quickly. The way things were going, there could have been yelling; I could have been thrown out of the house, sent packing. Instead, I am sitting in some shabby-chic living room with four new half-sisters and a stepsister, hearing about my loser dad. It's kind of surreal.

✿✿✿✿✿✿✿✿✿✿✿✿✿✿✿✿✿✿✿✿✿✿✿

'I almost knew,' Charlotte is saying now, her eyes on mine. 'When I heard your name, Jake, and saw your face, well, a shiver went down my spine. You look so like the girls, you see. So much like Greg. He was – is – a very handsome man.'

I wonder if it's too soon to ask to see a photograph and find out what my dad actually looks like. Maybe. In time. I bite my lip, tasting blood and hope.

'We've never had a brother before,' one of the twins says, a little less prickly now. 'Suppose it could be quite interesting.'

'Are you staying for tea?' the youngest sister asks. 'Because it's macaroni cheese and salad; me and Summer made it earlier. We made loads, so there will definitely be enough.'

'He lives in London, so he'll have to stay,' Honey declares. 'Besides, we are just getting to know him. He can't vanish again.'

'I am here, you know,' I cut in. 'You can't talk about me as if I'm not.'

'I'm sorry! I'm just so, *so* excited!' she exclaims, jumping down on to the floor beside me to drag me into another dramatic hug.

❀❀❀❀❀❀❀❀❀❀❀❀❀❀❀❀❀❀❀

'Put him down!' the littlest sister yelps. 'Honestly, Honey, you'll scare him to death!'

I wrestle myself free, exasperated, and Honey winks at me and rests her head on my shoulder. My eldest half-sister is impossibly full-on and probably insane; the twins are unexpectedly fierce; the littlest one seems friendly enough, but it does seem a little bit odd to be wearing a panda hat indoors in August. I think Paddy and Charlotte might be OK, though, and the dark-haired stepsister seems fine.

'I've texted Shay and told him not to come over,' she says now. 'He and Alfie were going to be in the filming, but all that will have to wait until tomorrow now. I figured we need a quiet evening in to talk and stuff.'

'That's exactly what we need,' Charlotte agrees.

'So you'll stay?' Paddy asks me, smiling. 'We can get the gypsy caravan made up for you.'

I have no idea at all what he is talking about, but I nod my head.

'Your mum's not expecting you back?' Charlotte presses.

I swallow, hard.

'No,' I say. 'Not really; she knew I was coming and she's totally fine with it . . .'

✿✿✿✿✿✿✿✿✿✿✿✿✿✿✿✿✿✿✿✿✿✿✿

The lie burns my tongue. A terrible compulsion to blurt out the truth boils up inside me, but I know it's a bad, bad idea. This family have never seen me before. They are nothing to do with me, really; we are connected by blood, by an accident of birth, but that doesn't make us family, no matter what Honey may think.

They do not need to hear my life story. They do not need to know my troubles – not yet anyhow. I am going to have to tread carefully to get this right.

'Great,' Paddy is saying. 'I might just give your mum a call, all the same. So she knows you arrived safely and everything. OK?'

'Sure,' I say, trying not to panic. 'Oh, she won't be in till later,' I lie. 'She's working a late shift at The Paper Dragon. She's a waitress, you see. Could you call tomorrow?'

'Tonight would be better,' Paddy says. 'What time does she finish?'

'Er, eleven?' I bluff. 'It really is quite late to be calling, so if you'd rather not . . .'

He shrugs. 'Not a problem. I'll call at eleven.'

'Great,' I say. 'Brilliant.'

Honey fixes me with a searching gaze. Can she tell I'm

lying? I think she can, but when she speaks she surprises me with a neat change of subject.

'So, Jake,' she says. 'Forget all that, just now. We want to know *everything* about you!'

I grin, saved for now at least, and rake a hand through my hair.

'For starters,' I say, 'You'd better call me Cookie . . .'

8

My little sisters are noisy enough, but the Tanberry-Costello lot? I have never met a family who talk so much. Every sister has an opinion, and every sister has about a million questions. They expect me to answer them all.

I tell them about Mum, Maisie and Isla, about the Paper Dragon restaurant, the train ticket and the fortune cookie that made me walk out of my life and come to Somerset. 'I was curious,' I explain. 'I wanted to meet you, see how I fitted in. It's like a whole load of jigsaw puzzle pieces were missing and I've found them – and now I can see the whole picture.'

As I say it, I realize this is true; I've been itching to meet my sisters since the second or third letter. I just didn't think I'd have the courage to do it; perhaps I never would have come, if it hadn't been for the Great Bathtub Disaster.

❀❀❀❀❀❀❀❀❀❀❀❀❀❀❀❀❀❀❀❀❀

And Tanglewood, well, it feels like a haven – a safe place to stay for a day or so, anyway. As long as Paddy doesn't ring Mum and mess the whole thing up, that is.

My life story does not include any mention of Sheddie with his dreadlocks, his t'ai chi and his moth-eaten yurt. It doesn't include my home- and restaurant-wrecking talents, or that my family will be evicted in a week's time. I don't mention that nobody knows where I am; or that I am, technically, a runaway. Why complicate matters?

The sisters show me photographs of my errant dad, and at last I get to see the man whose footsteps I am following in, the ultimate mess-up master. He is fair-haired and good-looking, tall and smiley and smartly dressed. There's a picture of his wedding to Charlotte, the two of them looking stupidly young and hopeful, and a series of pictures taken at a picnic where he sits on the grass with toddler-sized versions of the sisters draping themselves round him. The girls look scarily like me as a kid, just with longer hair. It's spooky.

I squint hard at the images of my dad; am I like him personality-wise, as well as in looks? Does he think about his life and wonder how it got to be so messed up? He doesn't look like trouble, but I know he is, of course. In the picnic photos he seems distant, distracted, as if his mind is else-where – as if he's already moving away from that perfect little family, moving on. I wonder how he'll react when I get in touch. Will he be glad to hear from me? Well, maybe, until he susses I'm after his cash.

We eat the macaroni cheese and salad from plates on our laps, and after a while the sisters talk endlessly about every single subject under the sun while plying me with home-made fruit smoothies and Paddy's amazing truffles, which are apparently famous. They are almost as good as a Snickers bar, possibly better.

By the time the clock is edging round towards eleven, I start getting jumpy again; if Paddy insists on ringing Mum my adventure could be over before it has properly started. My head is a muddle of half-baked plans and ideas. Could I text Harry or Mitch, ask if their mums would pretend to be mine? My mates would be onside, but I don't think their mums would. I could give a fake phone number but Paddy wouldn't be fooled by that for long. Whichever way I look at it, I'm in trouble.

'Hey,' Honey says, getting to her feet. 'Let me show you

the gypsy caravan, Cookie, so you know where you'll be sleeping!'

I follow her out through the kitchen, leaving the others engrossed in old photographs and memories. We slip out of the back door and down across the grass, Fred the dog at our heels, to where a brightly painted, bow-topped gypsy caravan is parked beneath trees draped with fairy lights. The light is fading fast and the air is cooler now; it is a million miles away from Chinatown and London.

'Cool,' I say. 'Weird, but cool.'

'Yeah, it's great,' Honey says flatly. 'But, look, something's going on, right? You were acting weird, sort of edgy, awkward, especially when Paddy was asking about your mum. Tell me if I'm wrong, but I don't think she knows you're here at all.'

I sigh. 'She doesn't,' I admit. 'It's a long story.'

Honey rolls her eyes in the twilight.

'So let's get this straight. You've run away?' she asks.

'Not exactly –'

'Have you or haven't you?' my half-sister demands.

'I suppose I have, kind of,' I say. 'I'm in trouble; well,

we're all in trouble, and it's my fault. I need to fix it, and to do that I need Dad's help.'

Honey laughs. 'Good luck with that,' she says. 'He's not exactly a fix-it kind of man, but hey. You can try. What are you going to do about Paddy? He's determined to speak to your mum.'

'He can't,' I tell her. 'That would ruin everything.'

'Won't she be worried?'

'Not really,' I explain. 'My little sister is covering for me. Mum thinks I'm staying with a friend.'

Honey nods, thoughtful. 'Clever,' she says. 'But not clever enough; you need to get Paddy off your trail.'

'How?' I ask. 'I can stall him for a while, but he doesn't look the kind of guy who'll give up. I'm stuffed, basically.'

Honey grins. 'Nah,' she says. 'I'll help you; it's simple, little brother. Have you got a mobile?'

I hand over my phone.

Honey sits down on the steps of the gypsy caravan.

'OK; so give Paddy this number,' she says, flicking open the mobile. 'I'll take the call. I'm doing drama at sixth-form college. I can do a mean cockney accent. Trust me!'

73

I don't trust Honey, not one bit, but I don't seem to have much choice.

I go back into the house. Paddy is in the kitchen making tea, and he looks up as I enter, smiling. 'Caravan OK for you?' he asks.

'Sure,' I say. 'It's amazing. Thanks!'

'Where's Honey?'

I think on my feet. 'She said she was taking Fred for a walk,' I say. 'I think she was texting someone. I didn't want to get in the way.'

Paddy nods. 'Her boyfriend is travelling in Europe,' he explains. 'They're communicating mostly by text. Not ideal, but he'll probably pitch up at Tanglewood before too long anyway. Speaking of communicating, Cookie, how about I call your mum now?'

I bite my lip. 'Yeah, yeah, no worries. Her name's Alison Cooke.'

I tell him my mobile number and keep my fingers crossed that Honey is telling the truth about her acting skill. I watch Paddy punch out the numbers, hear the call connect and listen to him telling the person on the other end that I've arrived safely and am welcome to stay for as long as I want to. There's a pause while he listens to the response, and my heart thumps. I must be crazy to imagine he'd be fooled by his own stepdaughter putting on a London accent, but to my amazement the conversation seems to run smoothly.

Moments later, Paddy holds the phone out to me.

'She wants a word,' he says.

I take the phone and watch as Paddy picks up two mugs of tea and heads back to the living room.

'So,' the cockney voice on the other end of the line says into my ear. 'That worked OK. I must be a better actress than I think.'

'My mum doesn't talk like that,' I say.

'She does now,' Honey says, dropping the accent abruptly. 'C'mon, Cookie, don't quibble.'

'I'm not,' I laugh. 'I'm amazed. Thank you, seriously. Just one question: why are you helping me?'

She laughs again. 'Because you're so like me,' she says. 'You're trouble, Cookie, pure and simple.'

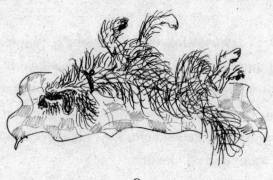

9

I wake up stupidly early, in a bunk in the funny little wooden caravan in the garden. I am cocooned in a patchwork quilt, my face pressed into a soft pillow that smells of fresh laundry. I stretch and yawn, and for a moment I panic because I can't move my legs, but this turns out to be because Fred the dog is lying on them. He is spreadeagled across the bunk like an extra blanket, an especially furry one.

'Hey, hey, bad dog!' I say, not really meaning it. 'Get down!'

Fred eyes me placidly and then rolls over again. I swear I can hear him snoring.

The caravan is tiny, but it's awesome. It has a little wood-burning stove, two windows with curtains, a brightly painted table and chair and a shelf with books. The roof curves up above my head and now that it's daylight I can see that every bit of wood is painted in rich, glossy shades of red, green and blue with patterns of swirling leaves and hearts and swooping birds worked in as decoration.

It's amazing. I could live somewhere like this, really I could.

I haven't had a room to myself since Manchester, and I am glad of a bit of space, a bit of quiet. It's cool. I think if you are going to discover a tenuous link to a mad family of half-sisters, they may as well live in an awesome house with a gypsy caravan and have a chocolate-making stepdad. Why not?

I push the curtain aside and peer out of the window; around the caravan sunlight filters through the trees and I catch a tantalizing glimpse of deep turquoise glinting in the distance.

That wedge of blue, can it be what I think it is?

I tumble out of bed, drag on the soy-sauce jeans and push open the caravan door. I stand on the caravan steps, taking in a few breaths of clean, cool air, and then I'm off across the dew damp grass, Fred the dog running ahead as I race towards the end of the garden.

77

And then I stop short, gazing out across the hedge.

An endless curve of turquoise lies before me, glittering in the watery morning sun, edged by a perfect crescent of golden sand.

Tanglewood House is right by the sea. How could I not have known? How could I not have guessed?

I unhook the rickety gate and run down the uneven cliff steps to the beach, my feet sinking into soft, cool sand, flinching as I dodge over sharp pebbles and shells. I am yelling by the time I reach the water's edge and run into the ice-cold turquoise waves, drenched to the skin and laughing. Fred the dog capers around beside me, barking.

I throw my head back to look at the perfect blue sky, the rising sun, and I only waste a tiny, tiny moment thinking of Maisie and Isla and how they would love this too.

None of us has ever been to the sea. Never, ever – not unless you count a day trip to Southend when I was a baby, and I have no memory of that at all, so I don't. I didn't know the sea would feel so big, so infinite. I didn't know the water would be so cold, so shocking. I didn't expect the taste of salt on my lips, the rush of blood through my body, the pounding of my heart, the laughter.

❀❀❀❀❀❀❀❀❀❀❀❀❀❀❀❀❀❀❀❀❀❀❀

For the first time in forever, I am fizzing with the joy of being alive.

'Hey! Cookie!'

I turn round and there is Honey, sitting on a rock at the foot of the cliff path, hand raised in greeting. Swallowing my pride at the thought of her watching me jumping waves and splashing about like a seal, I wade ashore and walk back over the sand with as much dignity as I can muster. Fred follows at my heels.

'Like it then?' Honey asks. 'It's cool having the sea on your doorstep. Stick around a bit; we'll throw a beach party in your honour, introduce you to everyone!'

'Well, I'm not planning on leaving just yet,' I say.

'Good. Because we have *so* much to catch up on; a whole lifetime of stuff! And that stupid film crew are pitching up at ten o'clock, and then I'll have to share you, and I don't want to, just yet. Not with a whole bunch of TV people anyhow.'

'What is it with that?' I ask. 'How come you're going to be on TV? Are you famous or something?'

Honey laughs. 'No, of course not; it's just one of those reality shows, a human interest sort of thing. We know the

✿✿✿✿✿✿✿✿✿✿✿✿✿✿✿✿✿✿✿✿✿✿✿

producer, Nikki, because she stayed at our house the summer before last – she was involved with a TV movie they were making in the village. I suppose they thought we'd be a good subject because we're a blended family, and that's very modern – and the whole chocolate thing gives it a bit of an edge.

'They've already shot most of the episodes, but they are always looking for drama and conflict and trouble, and I'm usually the main attraction there. I think they got more than they bargained for yesterday when you turned up!'

I blink. 'They won't use that clip, will they?' I panic. 'My mum would go nuts.'

Honey shrugs. 'Do you care? I mean, you ran away, right?'

'Not because I don't love my family,' I argue. 'I do. I told you, I'm in trouble and I need to put things right. I'm doing it *for* my mum, really.'

Honey raises an eyebrow. 'Interesting,' she comments. 'A hellraiser with a heart. Well, maybe your mum could come down to Tanglewood too, bring your little sisters? We could be one big, happy, deeply dysfunctional family.'

'I don't think so,' I mutter.

'No?' Honey huffs. 'I think it'd be brilliant. And the TV

❀❀❀❀❀❀❀❀❀❀❀❀❀❀❀❀❀❀❀❀❀

people could tell the whole story. Heart-warming, gripping stuff. Siblings reunited after a lifetime apart; two families brought together by their dislike of Greg Tanberry.'

'No,' I say. 'Not interested. And I don't think Charlotte would be too keen on the idea either . . .'

'Oh, Mum would come round,' Honey says airily. 'It would be *so* cool. But you're the boss; no worries. You're actually wanting to contact Dad, right?'

'I have my reasons,' I tell her. 'Trust me.'

'Never trust a fourteen-year-old boy who's just been jumping around in the sea fully dressed, that's my motto,' she quips. 'At the risk of sounding all big-sisterish and boring, I think you should probably go get changed. Otherwise the film crew really will be on your case, and *I* am the cool, eccentric one in this family, just so's you know!'

I look down at my dripping T-shirt and jeans, but before I can say anything Fred the dog gives himself a huge head-to-tail shake that splatters Honey with salt water. She squeals and swears and dodges out of the way, starting up the cliff steps again.

'He's as bad as you,' she says over her shoulder. 'Wretched thing. I can see this whole half-brother malarkey will take some getting used to – you'd think you'd never seen the sea before!'

'I haven't,' I reply, following. 'At least, not since I was six months old, and I can't remember much about that, funnily enough.'

Honey pushes through the gate and into the garden, her eyes wide.

'You've never seen the sea? Seriously?' She looks sad for a moment, as if trying to imagine my life and how different it has been from her own. Well, she can imagine all she likes, but she'll never come close to knowing. Sharing a tiny bedroom in a damp, scruffy flat with two little sisters while your mum kips on a sofa bed in the living room? Cooking up a culinary masterpiece with food-bank spam and a dented can of baked beans? These are challenges the Tanberry-Costello clan have never had to negotiate.

'Different strokes for different folks,' I say brightly, shutting the gate behind me. 'Don't feel sorry for me, OK? I bet you've never seen the sun set over the rooftops in Chinatown, or taken your sisters fishing by the Manchester Ship Canal. We didn't catch any fish, but we hooked a handbag, complete with purse and credit cards. We took it to the police station and got a £10 reward, but Maisie let slip to Rick and he was furious. Reckoned he could have used the cards to order a few thousand quids' worth of loot.'

'He doesn't sound very nice,' Honey says.

'He wasn't, really.'

Honey sighs. 'I hate that you've grown up so far away, and been through such difficult things. Our dad really does have a lot to answer for.'

And Honey doesn't know the half of it.

Who knows, maybe my dad sussed the situation pretty well. He heard about me and knew instinctively that I was going to be trouble. Who can really blame him for walking away from Mum, when he already had a sweet-natured wife, three pretty, clever daughters and another on the way, plus a rambling Victorian house right by the sea? The only thing I can't work out is why he chose to walk away from them as well, because if I'd had a set-up like Tanglewood I would never have let it go.

We walk up to the caravan together, my wet jeans squeaking a little. It takes me a moment to notice that a sheep is trailing along after us, and Honey tells me that this is Humbug, an orphan lamb that Coco raised from when she was a few days old. Humbug seems to think she is a dog, which is pretty surreal.

'Coco's got a pony too,' Honey says. 'Caramel. Check out the stables up by the chocolate workshop. Coco is a regular one-girl animal rescue!'

'My little sisters would love that,' I say. 'A dog, a sheep, a pony – cool!'

'Yeah, I guess. Got a girlfriend back in London?' Honey asks. 'I've got a boyfriend – I met him in Australia. I used to go for bad boy types, but Ash is . . . different. He's clever, studious, kind; not my usual type at all. And he kind of understands me, which nobody ever does, usually. I haven't seen him for ages, though.'

'Yeah? That sucks,' I comment.

'It really does,' Honey agrees. 'Just my luck to fall for a guy who lives on the other side of the planet. But he's finished school and he's been travelling – India, Sri Lanka – and now he's in Europe; Greece, apparently. Although I haven't heard from him for a couple of days now. I expect he's met some gorgeous gap year student and forgotten all about me.'

'More likely his phone's out of charge,' I say sensibly.

✿✿✿✿✿✿✿✿✿✿✿✿✿✿✿✿✿✿✿✿✿✿✿

'He's not going to forget about you, that's for sure. Are you planning to meet up?'

'Hopefully,' she says, and her eyes look misty and faraway all of a sudden. 'Might take him a month or so to work his way across Europe, but the idea is that he'll end up here. Maybe you'll meet him.'

'Maybe,' I say, although I know I will be long gone by then.

'So, girlfriend?' Honey presses. 'Are you a heartbreaker as well as a runaway, just like your big sister?'

I laugh out loud. 'Not exactly,' I admit. 'I haven't had a lot of time for romance, to be honest.'

'You will,' she says. 'You're not bad-looking, y'know, little brother! Although the dripping-wet look isn't really doing you any favours; you've brought a change of clothes, right?'

'Er . . . kind of.'

'OK. Get sorted and come up to the house; we'll grab some breakfast before the TV crew arrive.'

I turn and walk up the caravan steps, open the door.

'Cookie?' she says.

'Yeah?'

My half-sister grins in the dappled light beneath the trees, her blue eyes gleaming with pride.

❀❀❀❀❀❀❀❀❀❀❀❀❀❀❀❀❀❀❀❀❀❀

'It's just . . . I'm glad you came,' she says. 'I am a bit of a disaster zone as sisters go; I get stuff wrong, I mess things up, I always learn the hard way. I found out about you by accident, and I couldn't help it, I had to write. I wanted to see you, meet you. I wanted *you* to meet us. But – well, I was scared too. What if Mum freaked when she found out about you? What if my sisters blamed me, or if you hated us all? But it's going to be OK, Cookie, I know it is. I know you've rocked up here without telling anyone. I know you're on some mad mission to contact Dad, but so what? You're just . . . well, you're the perfect little brother. Looks like I finally got one thing right!'

She turns and runs up to the house, and I watch her go.

Nobody has ever described me as perfect before; I am about as far from perfect as it's possible to be. Honey knows I am a liar and a runaway but instead of judging me, she has taken it in her stride, kept her mouth shut, even helped me fake the phone call to Mum.

With a big sister like that, my plan can't fail.

10

If I'd thought that Tanglewood was crowded yesterday, today is something else. I am introduced to so many people my head starts to freeze; my eyes and ears can't take it all in.

There's Sandy, who manages the chocolate workshop, and her kids Lawrie and Jasmine. Lawrie is about my age, and he and Coco are practically inseparable, though possibly in a just-good-friends way. I can't quite tell. Then there's Alfie, Summer's boyfriend, who is freckled and funny and kind, and Shay, Cherry's boyfriend, who is clearly the guitar boy I was mistaken for yesterday. He is tall and fair and too-cool-for-school, with a knitted beanie hat (even though it's August) and an acoustic guitar slung over his back. And then there's two friends of the twins, Tia and Millie.

Over breakfast, Paddy and Charlotte reassured me that they'd called the producer and asked for the long-lost half-brother clip of film to be ditched.

'I told Nikki we need time to take the news in,' Charlotte explained. 'She totally understood. She asked if we could talk about it again in a week or so, when we've all had time to absorb the news a bit better, but I don't think I'll be changing my mind, Cookie. This is not the kind of thing I want broadcast across the nation, and I don't suppose you do either.'

I told her I definitely didn't.

The TV crew have a plan worked out for the day's filming. First, they will set up in the chocolate workshop to film Paddy and Charlotte making truffles; then they'll shoot Sandy taking a phone call about a rush order for a big department store, and everyone will be brought in to pack boxes and pull together. This was the scene my unexpected appearance scuppered last night, but the TV crew has re-imagined it, making it bigger and better, drafting in a cast of thousands. Or all these kids from the village anyhow.

The TV crew usher Charlotte, Paddy and Sandy over to the workshop to start filming while the village kids flop

❀❀❀❀❀❀❀❀❀❀❀❀❀❀❀❀❀❀❀❀❀❀❀

down round the kitchen table with the half-sisters. Summer brings a couple of pitchers of cloudy lemonade out of the fridge and pours glasses for everyone. People help themselves to toast and jam and talk non-stop about a million things and a million people I have never even heard of; they're more at home in the Tanglewood kitchen than I will ever be.

Summer hands me a glass of lemonade, complete with ice cubes and slice of lemon. I take a sip and almost choke; it's like no lemonade I've ever tasted before.

'What is that stuff?' I splutter. 'It's like paint stripper!'

'Not sweet enough for you?' Summer says. 'Sorry; I made it myself, and I like to give it a bit of a citrus kick. Think of all that vitamin C! It's really healthy, but you can add a bit more sugar if you want.'

I think the lemonade has taken a few layers of enamel off my teeth, but I just smile and shrug and abandon it on a window sill. The other kids seem to be drinking theirs all right; maybe country kids are used to sour, healthy, wince-making drinks with no fizz.

Honey seems to have forgotten me; she's right in the middle of the group, chatting easily, telling them all she's planning a beach party for her long-lost cousin and that they're all invited. I wonder who the cousin is, then realize it could be me.

Abruptly, I feel seriously homesick for our damp flat in Chinatown, for two annoying little sisters and a mum who works her socks off for us yet never seems to have a penny to show for it. She'd buy us proper lemonade, the supermarket fizzy kind. Mum has answered my text from yesterday with a breezy message telling me to come home soon; has she called Harry's mum to check up on where I am? Probably not, with Maisie covering for me. I have a track record of going missing from time to time, especially when I'm in trouble or when I've had some kind of blow-up with Mum. She knows to leave me be for a day or two, let me cool down. She knows I'll be back.

Having the freedom to head off and stay over at my friends is usually something I see as a good thing, but suddenly I feel angry, hurt; Mum will be busy right now tidying up the flat, getting ready for Sheddie's visit. She's probably glad I'm gone, out of her hair, not hanging around with a face like stone and a mouthful of cheek to fling at her ridiculous new boyfriend.

90

❀❀❀❀❀❀❀❀❀❀❀❀❀❀❀❀❀❀❀❀❀❀❀

Mum has no clue I've run away to clear my name, save The Paper Dragon and rescue us from homelessness, or, worse, a life of eating lentils and dandelion leaves in Sheddie's yurt.

She doesn't know I've tracked down my half-sisters. I don't even know if she's aware that they exist. I'm only just getting my own head around the fact that they're real. Their lives and mine are so very different that I know there's no way I can ever really be a part of all this; it's a fantasy, a daydream. A bit like the carefully planned TV show that's meant to look totally natural and random, things aren't quite the way they look on the surface, but still, Tanglewood is heaven compared to our flat in Chinatown.

I slip out of the door and back to the gypsy caravan, suddenly gloomy. I sink down on the caravan steps and turn my face up to the sun. Silence is a relief after the chaotic kitchen, but I can't forget why I'm here; it's not to socialize and it's not to have fun, it's to contact my dad and enlist his help.

It's lonely being a teenage superhero, especially when you are much more used to being a teenage tearaway, but I am determined. Once the film crew are gone, I will corner

Honey and get hold of Dad's email. I'm pretty sure she will agree to help. Meanwhile, curiosity and guilt about what might be happening back home gets to me, and I call Maisie.

'Maize?' I say as the call clicks through and the faint buzz of a vacuum cleaner fills my ears. 'It's me – shhh, pretend it's a friend, OK? Can you do the running-the-taps trick again?'

'Hello, Tara,' my little sister says, barely missing a beat. 'Great to hear from you. My mum is just hoovering the living room, *again*, so I am going to take this call in the bathroom.'

I hear a door slam and the sound of water running.

'All clear,' Maisie says. 'Mum is driving me mad. She hoovered twice yesterday and now she's at it again; how much cleaner can a place be?'

'She's stressed,' I explain. 'She always cleans when she's stressed. She'll be worrying about the bill for the ceiling and the bathroom.'

'She's worrying about Sheddie,' Maisie says. 'He's supposed to turn up later, in time for tea. We're having sausage and mash, only the sausages have got to be veggie because Sheddie doesn't eat meat.'

❀❀❀❀❀❀❀❀❀❀❀❀❀❀❀❀❀❀❀❀❀❀❀

'Great,' I say scornfully. 'He sounds grim. Don't worry, Maisie, I am working on a plan, and I am quietly confident I can save the day.'

'I've got a plan too,' Maisie says. 'Mum has told us we have to be on our best behaviour with Sheddie; that's what gave me the idea. Isla and me are going to be horrible to him. We're going to be rude and bad-mannered and spiteful. We're going to fight and yell and blank him if he tries to be nice to us. He won't want to live with us then.'

I start to laugh. Maisie is a genius, and her plot to drive Sheddie away might just help hold the fort until I get through to Dad and come up with a more lasting solution.

'Where are you, Cookie?' Maisie asks. 'Will you be back tonight?'

'Not tonight,' I tell her, Maybe tomorrow, or the day after. Can you keep Mum off my trail till then?'

'Definitely,' she says. 'But don't be away too long, OK?'

'I won't,' I promise. 'Thanks, Maisie, and good luck with Sheddie!'

I have a feeling she'll need it.

11

The peace and quiet doesn't last for long.

'You OK?' a voice asks, and one of the sisters appears through the trees, the one who isn't actually a sister at all. She has almond-shaped eyes and blue-black hair tied up in messy buns and red skinny jeans worn with a cool band T-shirt.

'Cherry?' I say, trying to remember her name.

'Yeah,' she says. 'That's right. I'm the stepsister, Paddy's daughter. Thought I'd see if you were OK – you looked a bit out of your depth back there. Tanglewood can be full-on at times.'

'Too many people,' I say. 'I'm still getting to know you lot – there's no chance of me coping with a whole new bunch of kids so soon. My brain just scrambles.'

Cherry smiles. 'I felt the same when I first arrived. It wasn't all that long ago, but it feels like I was a different person back then. I'd never seen anything like Tanglewood in my life.'

'Snap,' I say. 'It's like a castle or something, well, a slightly shabby one. But – I dunno, it's like magic. The caravan, the beach, the sea.'

'I slept in the caravan too, when I first came,' she tells me. 'Charlotte was running the house as a B&B back then so the place was always manic; the caravan was my bolt-hole.'

'Yeah, I can see how that would work,' I say.

'I lived in Glasgow before we came here,' she goes on. 'We had a little flat in a tenement building. Dad worked in a chocolate factory, sweeping the floor, and I was really miserable . . . probably the most unpopular girl in my school. Tanglewood really must be magic, Cookie, because it changed all that.'

My eyes widen. 'Your dad swept the floor in a factory?' I check. 'And now he's running a business so successful that the TV are making a reality TV show about him? I thought, well, I assumed you were like the Tanberry girls. Y'know, a rich kid with a perfect life.'

95

Cherry sits down on a fallen tree trunk, regarding me carefully.

'Well, I'm not,' she says. 'I'm just ordinary. A kid from Glasgow with a big imagination and not enough common sense. The others are just ordinary too. I suppose I thought they had everything when I first came, but that's not true. It's not the way it looks.'

I frown. 'How come?'

'Well, the house is gorgeous, but it doesn't exactly belong to us,' Cherry begins. 'Charlotte's mum inherited it, but she remarried and lives in France now. Most of the sisters were born here, but after Greg – your dad – left them, Charlotte really struggled. Greg didn't pay any maintenance, or not much, and not regularly. Like I said, she ran the place as a B&B.'

'Great guy my dad has turned out to be.' I shrug. 'Still, it's good to know his mean streak was fair and across the board, and not just aimed at Mum and me. If you know what I mean.'

She sighs. 'I know what you mean.'

'So OK, I'm not saying the Tanberrys are rich . . .'

'Just privileged?' Cherry teases. 'Well, maybe. It's a

different life from the one we were used to, sure. Don't think everything's been easy for your half-sisters, though – it hasn't. Honey was totally off the rails before she went to Australia. She ran away a few times; the last time she took her passport and a load of money out of the kitchen drawer and the police picked her up at Heathrow, trying to book a ticket to see her dad in Sydney.'

'The police?' I echo, trying not to sound impressed. 'Wow!'

'Not wow, not really,' Cherry tells me. 'The social workers almost took her into care. And then while she was in Australia she got cyberbullied really badly. She looks confident, but – well, she's a bit of mess.'

I nod, chastened. I hadn't imagined that Honey's rebellious streak ran quite that deep; maybe I have more in common with her than I thought.

Mum has always impressed on me that I have to keep a lid on my troublemaker tendencies. 'If you keep breaking the rules, they'll take you away from me,' she said once, when we were still in Manchester and I was getting into a lot of trouble in school. 'I'm a single parent family, Cookie. They'll think I'm not coping.' I'd tried very hard after that to avoid kicking off. I didn't want to lose my mum, my sisters.

97

'Then there's Summer,' Cherry is saying. 'Two years ago she had auditions for one of the most prestigious boarding ballet schools in the country; being a dancer had always been her dream. She put herself under so much pressure she fell to bits, pretty much. She's been attending the eating disorder clinic ever since. She's much stronger now, but – well, not so perfect, huh?'

I think of Summer's sad blue eyes, her graceful bird-like frame, and I begin to understand. 'Anorexia,' I say, piecing the story together. 'That's bad, isn't it?'

'It could have killed her,' Cherry says. 'As it is, it derailed her hopes and dreams. She was on track to be a professional dancer, but she just couldn't handle the pressure.'

'That sucks. Poor Summer.'

'Yeah. Skye and Coco are OK. Skye's mad on vintage and history, and Coco is animal crazy and wants to save the world. They're both really kind and cool and fun, though.'

'And how about you?'

'I'm good,' Cherry grins. 'I don't tell whopping great lies any more, or throw my dinner over people's heads – not recently anyhow.'

I grin. 'Yikes. I'll watch my step with you around then!'

❀❀❀❀❀❀❀❀❀❀❀❀❀❀❀❀❀❀❀❀❀❀

'Do that,' she says. 'I wouldn't want to go having a relapse; although actually you might suit a plate of macaroni cheese in the hair.'

She keeps a straight face for all of ten seconds, and then the two of us are laughing out loud. I think Cherry probably understands how I'm feeling better than anyone – she has been an outsider here too, after all.

'C'mon, come back in for the filming,' she coaxes. 'If I can do it, you can do it. It won't be so bad, honest.'

'It will be,' I scowl. 'I don't know how you stick it, having those TV people crawling around everywhere. Have they got secret cameras in the loo as well?'

'Hope not,' Cherry laughs. 'It's funny – everybody wants to get in on the filming, grab their fifteen minutes of fame, but it's not my idea of fun. I'm more of a behind-the-scenes kind of girl, but we all have to be in it; it'd look odd otherwise. And it'll be great publicity for Dad and Charlotte, so nobody really minds. Nikki, the producer, knows Dad and Charlotte pretty well; we trust her not to put together something dodgy. She knows how she wants the storyline to pan out.'

I pull a face. 'Honey was saying. That's strange, right? I

mean, it's supposed to be reality TV, but it isn't, is it? It's all scripted. Fake.'

She frowns. 'Not exactly scripted; we get to say what we want to. The stuff we're filming, like this rush order thing today, did actually happen. It's just that it was a while ago. They play around with the facts a bit, trying to make good TV. There's a kind of storyline they've worked out with Mum and Paddy, ending up with the Chocolate Festival.'

'The what?'

'It's something we did a couple of years ago as part of a local food trail,' Cherry explains. 'It was back when we launched the chocolate business. The TV people want us to do it again, like a grand finale for the series. It's next Saturday. The whole village will probably be up here for that – maybe you can stick around?'

I shrug, trying to seem non-committal, but I do not plan to be here in a week's time. By then I hope I'll have persuaded Dad to cough up some cash to do the repairs on The Paper Dragon. The alternative is grim: a yurt in Millford. It doesn't bear thinking about.

I could always keep running, I suppose. By next Saturday I could be hitch-hiking my way across Albania. The six

✿✿✿✿✿✿✿✿✿✿✿✿✿✿✿✿✿✿✿✿✿✿✿

o'clock news could be reporting on my mysterious disappearance; they'd flash up my last school photo, a hideous shot of me in a crumpled shirt with too-long hair, looking about eleven. Not good. Maybe they'd do an interview, with Mum crying and Gran saying what a great kid I was, and Sheddie lurking in the background looking guilty and knowing it was all his fault.

It's unlikely, though. Mum would probably just be cross and Gran might tell the cameras that I'd always been trouble, exactly like my no-good father. Maybe they'd be better off without me. They'd forget me in the end, or learn to remember me fondly: the rebellious kid who vanished in the night to seek his fortune and build a life that didn't involve yurts and nettle soup.

'Maybe your mum and sisters could come down for it?' Cherry is saying. 'The Chocolate Festival?'

'Maybe not,' I mutter.

She raises an eyebrow. 'Don't get on with them?' she asks. 'What happened?'

I sigh. I suppose I could set the scene a little; tell her about Sheddie, who even now may be trudging through London in his hand-plaited hippy sandals, on his way to the flat to charm my mum and my little sisters with his stupid home-grown vegetables and his pathetic t'ai chi. I could tell her about Mr Zhao, whose restaurant I destroyed almost single-handedly, or Gran who chose to catch the tube and not the bus and so arrived too late to save the day.

Or I could cut to the chase and tell her about Mum, working herself to death in her black silk cheongsam dress, carrying plates of wonton soup and egg-fried rice and dreaming of better things. I could explain how Isla abandoned her bathtub Barbie swimming pool in favour of Jammie Dodgers and a go on the swings at the park, how even now Maisie is holding the fort and hatching her plan to freeze out Sheddie.

I could tell her that this time next week, we will technically be homeless, and all because of me.

I look at Cherry, and wonder if I can trust her.

'It's a long story,' I begin. 'But . . . well, I've kind of run away from home.'

12

Before I can say any more, a voice rings out through the
bright morning air.

'Cookie? Where are you?' Honey comes through the
trees, Fred the dog and Humbug the sheep at her heels.
The moment is lost. 'Why are you hiding away out here?
Oh – Cherry! What are *you* doing here?'

'We were talking,' I say, jumping down from the caravan
steps. 'I've been hearing all about your misspent youth.'

Honey's smile slips and vanishes, and I know I've put my
foot in it again. 'What have you been saying?' she demands
of Cherry. 'You've got no right to go telling tales; my life
is none of your business, believe it or not!'

Cherry sighs. 'I didn't,' she whispers. 'I just . . . it
was only –'

'Hang on,' I cut in. 'I was joking, Honey! Winding you up! You told me yourself you were a troublemaker. I didn't need Cherry to tell me that. We were just chatting, seriously, about the TV crew and the chocolate business.'

I'm rambling now, but Honey's expression softens and she shoots a guilty look at Cherry. 'OK,' she says. 'Fine. Whatever. Just – kind of a sore point, Cookie. You weren't to know. Um . . . sorry, Cherry . . .'

'No worries,' Cherry says in a small voice, but she can't meet Honey's eye and I wonder just what I've raked up with my clumsy joke. There's definitely a vibe of hostility between the two girls. Cherry might be right – things are not quite as perfect at Tanglewood as they seem.

'Anyway,' Honey is saying. 'The film crew are ready for the rush order scene with all of us in it; they're setting up the lights in the kitchen right now, so come on – you're not allowed to wriggle out of it! The make-up girl is trying to put face powder on Alfie; he is *so* not impressed! Wait till they get their hands on you, Cookie; this is going to be so cool!'

It's the furthest thing from cool I can possibly imagine, but I fix a smile on my face, promise to give it my best shot and follow Honey and Cherry up to the house.

❀❀❀❀❀❀❀❀❀❀❀❀❀❀❀❀❀❀❀❀❀

Packing chocolates into boxes with a whole crowd of crazy kids while a film crew watch our every move is one way to get to know the locals, I suppose. By the time we're done with filming, I know all about Alfie's taste in cheesy jokes, about Lawrie's rescued fox with only three legs who is almost tame, about Shay's dreams of musical stardom and lots more.

There are a few scripted bits: shots of Paddy, Charlotte and Sandy saying they despair, that even if they can get the chocolates made in time there is no way they will ever get everything packed up and ready to dispatch, then a shot of Honey on the phone, asking an imaginary person on the other end to come over and help, and bring anyone else they can think of.

After that, they film us all trudging up to the house across the gravel as the family welcome us with hugs and exclamations that we've saved their bacon. 'I don't have any bacon,' Coco says. 'I'm vegetarian. Bacon is actually just a murdered pig.'

I have a feeling the TV people might edit that bit out, but I suppose you never know.

After that we troop into the kitchen and the clipboard

woman arranges us round the kitchen table so she can see everybody's face. We have to tie ribbon bows round chocolate boxes and pack them up into crates, which is hardly strenuous; we also get to chat, which helps a little. I am enjoying my secret life as the Tanberrys' imaginary long-lost cousin; seriously, if I'd known acting could be this much fun, I might have showed up at a few more drama lessons at school.

And hey, I am practically a TV star now.

It gets a little unsettling when the cameras zoom in close and the mics hover above our heads, and Shay is asked to sing some of his songs while sitting on the draining board of the kitchen sink. 'Look natural,' the clipboard lady tells him. 'Relax. You're just entertaining your friends while they work – an impromptu concert.'

Shay smiles and shrugs and tries to chill, but I don't think anybody can relax while perched on a draining board and at one point he knocks the Fairy Liquid off the side and into the washing-up bowl with the top of his guitar, and they have to stop filming and do another take. He has a good voice, though, and the songs have a gentle indie-folk vibe that's pretty cool.

'He's good,' I tell Cherry under my breath. 'I thought

he was just spinning a line about wanting to be a musician, but he's easily good enough for *X Factor*.'

Cherry laughs. 'Not sure if he'd be into that, but yeah, he's good,' she whispers back. 'He wrote a track that got used in a TV film last year; this could be another break for him. When we do the Chocolate Festival he's going to do a set there as well. Not sitting in the sink, obviously.'

'Awesome,' I say.

Finally the filming is finished and the TV crew pack up. The box-packing party disintegrates and the props are cleared away, but nobody seems inclined to leave; Honey mentions her impromptu beach party idea again, and everyone seems up for that. The sisters heat up pizzas to share and someone conjures up coleslaw and salad out of thin air just about, but luckily the sour lemonade has all gone so we have to make do with squash.

Everything is ferried down to the beach and the afternoon unfurls around me like some cool screenplay I have somehow managed to blag myself a bit part in. We sit around on blankets and rugs, eating and chatting and soaking up the sun, and just as I'm digging into the fruit salad, Coco and the twins stand up to make some kind of speech.

'We are gathered here today, in the sight of – well, just you guys, really,' Coco begins. 'But it's a gorgeous day and we wanted to do something cool to welcome our long-lost –'

'Cousin,' Honey cuts in, shooting me a meaningful look. 'Our long-lost *cousin*.'

'That's what I was going to say,' Coco huffs. 'Obviously!'

A few of the village kids exchange puzzled looks, but it looks like strange happenings and unexpected cousins are par for the course at Tanglewood, because everybody goes along with it.

'Not all of you will be aware of this,' Skye picks up the story. 'But until yesterday, most of us didn't know anything at all about Cookie. And then he turned up out of nowhere, and it was all a bit of a shock, but we wanted to throw this party to let him know – to let *you* know, Cookie – that we are just really, really happy to have you as part of our family!'

Skye goes a little pink and tries to hide behind her hair, and her twin takes over the speech.

'The thing is that you can never have too many cousins,' Summer says carefully. 'So we are very glad indeed to welcome you to Tanglewood, and we hope you can stay for a while and get to know everyone. It's just – well, really cool to find out we're related. So, yeah. That's it, really!'

I feel all warm and fuzzy inside, touched that the sisters are making an effort to welcome me. The smile on my face is about a mile wide.

Coco, the youngest sister, edges her way forward again.

'I now declare this beach party *open*!' she announces, and Shay picks up his guitar and Alfie starts a ramshackle football match and eventually just about everybody heads into the sea for a swim. My jeans are still at that slightly crispy stage of drying out after this morning's unplanned dip, so I am not keen to join in. I pretend to be chilling in the sunshine instead.

'Hey, little brother, how d'you like our welcome party?' Honey asks. 'Sorry for demoting you to cousin status; we figured you might prefer it that way. It's nobody's business but ours, is it? This is all a bit last minute, obviously, but there'll be a party on Saturday night, after the Chocolate Festival too; it's going to be epic!'

'I'll be gone by then,' I tell her sadly.

Honey frowns. 'How come?' she wants to know. 'You've run away, right? It's not like you have somewhere better to be.'

'It's complicated. I can't really explain right now, but I will, I promise. It's just that I don't have much time and I can't get sidetracked with, well, fun and stuff.'

'Why not? It's a Sunday afternoon in August and you're on the best little beach in Somerset; enjoy it!'

I laugh. 'I will, honest. I just keep worrying about stuff, that's all. I should get in touch with Dad now I know who he is. Let him know I exist and all that . . .'

'We'll have to Skype him, introduce him to his long-lost son,' Honey agrees. 'Although that might actually scare him to death; maybe a phone call first, or an email?'

'I'll email,' I say. 'There's quite a lot I need to say to him, and I want to give him time to take it in. I just need the email address.'

'Sure,' Honey agrees. 'Just one thing; you know how I didn't get round to telling Mum and the sisters that I'd found you? Well, I didn't tell Dad either. His girlfriend let it slip when she was upset – she used to be his secretary, and she'd dealt with some paperwork when he made a payment to your mum when you were born.'

I nod, trying to take this all in.

'I didn't find out for sure until the night before I flew

❀❀❀❀❀❀❀❀❀❀❀❀❀❀❀❀❀❀❀❀❀

home,' Honey is saying. 'I went searching through his study and I found an old briefcase with some papers about you. I didn't tell Dad I knew; he'd have been really angry, and things were already rocky between us by then. Does that make sense?'

'Sure, no worries,' I reply. 'I'd rather do this on my own, anyway. It's between me and him; no need for you to get involved.'

The relief is clear on Honey's face. I can see how much she needs her dad's approval, even now that she knows he's a very long way from perfect. I hate him, just for a minute, for all the hurt and chaos he has left in his wake.

I hand Honey my mobile and she taps in the email address for me. My fingers shake as I take the mobile back. I want to email right now, but this is not the time or the place. Plus, there's that whole time-zone thing – I can afford to be patient; the other side of the planet is still sleeping.

I look out towards the ocean, my eyes on the horizon where it curves away from me, stretching onwards to a whole world beyond my imagining. A world where my dad is waiting.

'Changed your mind about the water?' Honey asks,

❀❀❀❀❀❀❀❀❀❀❀❀❀❀❀❀❀❀❀❀❀❀

misreading my thoughts. 'Roll your jeans up and paddle.' In the end I do just that, because the sand is scorching and the turquoise glint of sea is irresistible. I kick off my trainers and tuck my mobile down into the toe of one of them, rolling up my jeans as far as they'll go.

As I wade into the water, the boys descend on me for a water fight, and in two minutes flat I'm on my knees, drenched from head to toe, firing off swear words in between torrents of laughter. It's one of those bonding moments; it's hard to explain, but I somehow know that Shay, Alfie and Lawrie and the other kids are OK people. I have already gathered that much about Honey, Coco, Skye, Summer and Cherry, as well as Paddy and Charlotte. Spending a few days lying low in Somerset is not exactly going to be a hardship.

The air smells of coconut suncream and salty water and summer, and I try not to think of Isla and Maisie and how much they would love this, how they'd whoop and scream and crash through the surf and build sandcastles with moats and turrets and shells. I try not to think of them back home at the flat, giving Mum's new boyfriend the silent treatment as he tries to charm them into a future of yurt-living and lentil stew.

✿✿✿✿✿✿✿✿✿✿✿✿✿✿✿✿✿✿✿✿✿

As the afternoon melts into evening, Alfie, Lawrie and Coco build a makeshift bonfire, and the smell of woodsmoke drifts on the breeze and adds to the magic.

Summer asks me if I have ever been to the Royal Ballet at Covent Garden, or to Sadler's Wells, and I have to admit I've never even been to the cinema in London, let alone anything arty or cultural. Then Skye tries to pick my brains about London vintage shopping, and I pretend to know what she's talking about. I'm guessing she doesn't mean charity shops or jumble sales, although you never know. Coco chimes in to tell me how global warming is melting the polar ice cap and everyone should go vegetarian, and I tell her my mum's new boyfriend is a veggie t'ai-chi-teaching willow weaver with waist-length dreadlocks and she says he sounds nice, which just about kills the conversation dead.

I guess it takes all sorts.

In the end, I strip off my soaked T-shirt, slather on some suncream and weasel my way on to a corner of the picnic blanket Cherry and Shay are sharing. I lie back and shut my eyes and listen to Shay's guitar, and for an hour or two at least, I try not to think of anything at all.

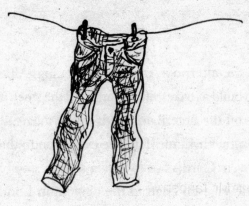

13

I end up having to borrow a pair of Paddy's checked PJ trousers with a belt tied round them because they're too big, while my jeans go in the washing machine overnight to wash away the salt and the sand. Next morning I go to rescue them and find that the soy-sauce stain has vanished too, and I feel strangely sad, like a little part of my old life has been washed away.

The house is silent and still, the breakfast things still stacked up on the draining board, like everyone has been called away urgently; I feel like an intruder, helping myself to cereal and fruit. I wash the dishes, just to be helpful; I don't want the Tanberry-Costello gang to think I am taking them for granted.

Later, I hang the jeans on the cherry tree by the gypsy

caravan to dry, and they flutter a little in the morning breeze, like a medieval pennant.

It's 11.32 a.m. British time, and I am still waiting for a reply to the email I sent to Greg Tanberry last night.

Dear Mr Tanberry,

I know this is going to come as a shock to you, but hey, not as much of a shock as it was to me. I am writing because I have just found out I am your son. Don't worry about how I found out; you don't need to know that. You just need to know that my mum's name is Alison Cooke and that she worked for you fourteen or fifteen years ago, and I expect you know the rest so I am not going to spell it out. Anyway, my name is Jake Cooke and I am fourteen years old, and I suppose you know that too. I am still getting to grips with the whole idea of having a dad, even if it is a dad on the other side of the world. I have a lot to say to you and a favour to ask, if that's OK, but for now I guess that just saying 'hi' is a start.

Hope to hear from you soon.

Yours faithfully,
Jake Cooke

❀❀❀❀❀❀❀❀❀❀❀❀❀❀❀❀❀❀❀❀❀❀❀

I check my email for about the seventieth time – still no reply. I tell myself to be patient, then click refresh just in case a reply has arrived in the last thirty seconds. Nothing.

'Hey, Cookie!'

Cherry is walking down through the trees, a supermarket carrier bag swinging over her arm, two glasses of orange juice with ice in her hands.

'Hey,' I say. 'I wondered where everyone was; the house was deserted earlier. What's going on?'

'Just your average summer holiday Monday,' she says with a shrug. 'Honey's still in bed, Paddy's in the chocolate workshop, Coco's taken Caramel for a beach trek and Charlotte drove into Minehead first thing to drop Summer at dance class. She spent the whole of last week there, helping out at a summer school for the younger kids – she was a kind of student teacher. You'd think she'd have had enough of it, but no, she's back again, for her senior class. Skye went into town too, to meet Millie and Tia, and Charlotte and I did a big supermarket shop. We got some bits for you, actually.'

'Me?'

'Just a couple of things that might be useful,' she says, chucking the carrier bag into my arms. 'You're travelling light; we thought that if you were staying a day or so, you might need some more clothes.'

I look in the bag and bring out two plain brightly coloured T-shirts, a pair of skinny jeans, board shorts, boxers and a pair of flipflops. They are all bargain-basement cheap, but still, I don't like the idea of Charlotte shelling out her cash for me.

'Aw, no,' I argue. 'I don't need all this. Charlotte didn't have to do this. I can't repay her, I've only got seven pounds and ninety-two pence to my name!'

'She doesn't want you to repay her,' Cherry says. 'It's a prezzie – and don't panic, there was a sale on, so everything was marked down. At least you won't have to mooch around in Paddy's pyjama bottoms. Not being funny, but that is not a good look.'

'No?' I query, tugging at the billowing tartan fabric. 'I thought they were pretty rad myself, but what do I know? Seriously, thanks for all this. All the right sizes too – how did Charlotte know?'

'She checked your jeans when she washed them,' Cherry explains. 'I looked inside your trainers at the beach yesterday, and we just guessed with the T-shirts.'

❀ ❀

'Cool,' I say. 'How do I thank Charlotte? Pick some flowers or something? Mow the lawn? I'd like to do something useful, show I'm grateful for how you've all made me welcome.'

'Well, there are a few things still to do for the Chocolate Festival,' Cherry tells me. 'Decorations to sort, food to make, a marquee coming on Thursday that needs all hands on deck to put up, that kind of thing. Dad was talking about making a stage for the musicians, something makeshift under the trees, but I don't think he'll have time now. He'll be in the workshop all week making sure there's enough stock. It won't matter about the stage; we didn't have one last time.'

'I could make one,' I volunteer. 'I'm actually OK at woodwork. Design tech is one of my best subjects at school.'

It's the only subject I bother to turn up for most of the time, but I don't tell Cherry that. We walk through the trees together and Cherry shows me where Paddy planned to make his DIY stage.

'Shay will be playing, obviously,' she tells me. 'But we've invited a few other local acts along too. Having a stage would make it special; give a focal point to the festival. D'you really think you could do something? It doesn't have to be fancy.'

'I'm on it,' I tell her. 'Do you have any stuff I could use? Old packing cases, wood offcuts?'

'There's a whole storeroom full of pallets and crates and bits of hardboard next to Caramel's stable,' Cherry says. 'You can use any of that. I expect Dad'd be really pleased if you could cobble something together, even if it was pretty basic.'

'Leave it with me.'

Cherry perches on a tree stump, sipping her orange juice.

'So was that true, what you told me yesterday?' she asks. 'About running away?'

I frown. 'Might have been.'

'But I don't get it. Dad said he spoke to your mum.'

I grin. 'He didn't,' I say. 'I gave him my mobile number, not Mum's, and Honey sat out here and took the call. She put on a cheesy cockney accent and your dad totally fell for it.'

Cherry's eyes widen. 'That is so typical of Honey,' she says. 'I bet she loved putting one over on Dad. Still, it

❀❀❀❀❀❀❀❀❀❀❀❀❀❀❀❀❀❀❀❀❀❀❀

worked, didn't it? And nobody knows you're a runaway except me and Honey. Wow.'

'You can't tell anybody,' I say. 'Promise?'

She sighs. 'I won't give you away, Cookie, I promise. I'm guessing you have your reasons.'

'You could say that.'

Cherry is surprisingly easy to talk to for a stepsister I've barely met. Her eyes widen as I describe the restaurant waterfall and the ruined bathroom fenced off with orange plastic tape. Only once does she interrupt, to say, 'Oh, cool,' when I mention the bit about Sheddie and living in a yurt.

'Not cool,' I correct her, and she frowns and nods.

'No, of course not,' she agrees. 'Not if that's not your choice. I'm sorry.'

So I carry on, explaining how Mr Zhao is closing The Paper Dragon and putting us all out on the street. 'That's why she's decided to move in with Sheddie,' I explain. 'She thinks we have no choice!'

'Did you ask her?' Cherry questions. 'Are you sure that's why she wants to move?'

'No, but it has to be that, surely?' I say. 'No restaurant, no job, no flat and suddenly this hippy-dippy weirdo comes on the scene. I mean, she never even mentioned him until after the flood. Don't tell me it's all a coincidence, Cherry. It can't be!'

'It does sound worrying,' Cherry concedes. 'I can see why you're concerned but I still don't get why you've run away. Why come here now, just when your family need you most? I'm glad you did, don't get me wrong, but how can that solve anything?'

I explain my idea of emailing Dad to ask for the money to repair the damage and help set us on an even keel again.

'He owes it to us, really,' I say. 'One payment, my mum had from him, just after I was born. Mum says it was all gone by the end of the year. And after that – no maintenance, nothing to help at all.'

'He did the same to Charlotte, I think,' Cherry says. 'Dad says Greg promised weekly payments. He was legally obliged to make them, but they hardly ever came through. Charlotte and the girls were living hand-to-mouth when we moved in. The B&B made enough money for them to live on, but there was never anything to spare. Dad and Charlotte got a loan to start the Chocolate Box business and thankfully it's really taken off.'

❀❀❀❀❀❀❀❀❀❀❀❀❀❀❀❀❀❀❀❀

I sigh. 'Paddy's OK,' I say. 'He's kind, yeah? My dad, not so much.'

'Have you made contact yet?'

'I've emailed but he hasn't answered,' I admit. 'He's probably checking me out, working out if I am who I say I am. Or maybe he just hopes I'll go away. I won't, though. I can't. I have to hope he has a little bit of goodness in him.'

'It's not his most obvious quality,' she says. 'I suppose he might just have a conscience, though – and he does owe you. Good luck with the plan, Cookie. Just don't be too upset if it doesn't work out, OK?'

'It will work out,' I argue. 'It has to. You don't understand, Cherry – I have to put things right!'

Cherry tilts her head to one side, thoughtful.

'You actually think all of this is your fault, don't you?' she asks. 'You're taking the blame. And that's crazy; it was an accident!'

I shake my head. 'It was my fault,' I say. 'I was left in charge – I messed up. I made the wrong decisions and I've wrecked everything, but I am not like my dad, Cherry. I'm not going to walk away from it all, I'm going to face up to it, take responsibility, fix it.'

❀❀❀❀❀❀❀❀❀❀❀❀❀❀❀❀❀❀❀❀❀❀

'That's really cool,' she says. 'I really admire what you're doing. But I still don't think any of it was your fault!'

I shrug a little sadly. 'I wish you were right, but – well, I know it was. Besides, I think it's fate the way the rail ticket Honey sent me and the fortune cookie I got from Mr Zhao two years ago just happened to fall off the wall at that particular moment. It had to be a sign, right?'

Cherry bites her lip.

'Maybe,' she says. 'I hope so. So your mum doesn't know where you are at all?'

'It's fine.' I shrug. 'She thinks I'm staying with my mate Harry. My little sister Maisie is covering for me and I've gone AWOL before, for a day or two at any rate. She won't be worried.'

I cross my fingers as I say it. Hopefully Mum will be so tied up with Sheddie's visit that my disappearance will take a back seat – for a while, anyway. And by the time she starts asking awkward questions, I should have the cash from Dad and all our troubles will be over. I hope.

I can see that Cherry is sceptical, though.

'I have to try,' I tell her. 'And Dad is my only option. I feel bad for Mr Zhao. I know he's mad with me – with all of us – but I can't let him evict us, can I? And I can't let Mum hook up with this Sheddie person for all the wrong reasons. How would you like to live in a yurt with some creep you've never even met before?'

'I wouldn't,' Cherry says staunchly. 'I can see why you're upset. I'll help you if I can, but I really think you should confide in Dad and Charlotte. They'd know what to do. They'd help you, really.'

I shake my head, vehement.

'Not happening,' I say firmly. 'Paddy and Charlotte are great, but I really don't want to talk to them about this. Besides, adults never actually help on things like this; they wade in and stir things up and everything ends up a million times worse than it was in the first place. They wouldn't get it. They'd call Mum and she'd go nuts and stop me getting hold of Dad, and we'd be back at square one again. So thanks, but no thanks. I can't tell them – and nor can you, Cherry, OK? You promised.'

She nods. 'I know I did,' she says, standing up, gathering up the empty glasses. 'And I keep my promises, don't worry. I won't tell anyone, not even Shay. Look – I also promised Dad I'd help out in the chocolate workshop this afternoon.

✿✿✿✿✿✿✿✿✿✿✿✿✿✿✿✿✿✿✿✿✿✿

Give us a shout if you decide to do something about making a stage. Maybe Alfie or Shay or Lawrie would come up and help you.'

'I'll have a think,' I say. 'It might stop me worrying whether my dad's ever going to reply.' I force a smile, but my heart is heavy.

What if I really am kidding myself?

She grins. 'It'll be OK, Cookie. It has to be,' she says.

I hope she's right.

14

Once Cherry's gone, I check my mobile again to see if Dad has replied. He hasn't, but there's a text from Maisie asking me to call and another from Mum, telling me she knows I'm taking some time out but that she really hopes I'll come home soon because everyone is missing me like mad and we are supposed to be moving on Saturday, so vanishing off the face of the earth is not the smartest thing I have ever done.

Just wait until I return with the cash to sort everything out, to rescue The Paper Dragon and save us from a life of homelessness, or – worse – life with Sheddie. We'll see then who's smart.

I don't say any of that in the end.

I'll come back soon. I text. **Once your stupid boyfriend's gone.**

It's kind of mean, I know, but I am not in the mood to pretend to be impressed by a dreadlocked t'ai chi teacher. Why are Mum's choices of boyfriend always so disastrous? I press 'send'.

I call Maisie, and she answers on the first ring.

'Hello, Tara!' she says, practised now at lies and subterfuge and clearly getting away with murder too; the 'emergency only' mobile is now clearly being used much more. 'I was hoping you'd call. Guess what? We're at the zoo!'

'What?' I falter. 'The zoo? What's going on?'

'Hang on, Tara,' she says in a too-loud voice. 'I'm just going to go and sit over by the penguins, because they are my favourite thing. We're having the best day ever, I swear! I think the others are going to get ice cream; can I have a 99 please? With strawberry sauce?'

'What others?' I ask. 'Who are you with?'

'Mum and Isla, of course,' she reports. 'And Sheddie. He's really cool, Cookie. You'd like him!'

'I would not like him!' I argue, outraged. 'Maisie, can they hear you? Be careful!'

'They're getting ice creams,' she says. 'It's a really long queue. Don't worry!'

'Don't worry?' I echo. 'Of course I'm worried! What happened to the plan to freeze Sheddie out and make him hate you?'

'Oh, that,' Maisie says scornfully. 'It didn't work, because he is actually really nice. He asked us what we wanted to do for a special day out, and we said the zoo, and so we're here! Although he says he doesn't really believe in zoos, he prefers in-the-field conservation projects. He's going to help me and Isla sponsor a tiger through some wildlife charity; you get a signed picture and a cuddly toy. Isn't that cool?'

'He's the enemy,' I remind Maisie. 'Don't go getting all friendly with him, he wants to take us all to live in some mouldy tent in Milltown, remember?'

'I've seen a picture, and it's not mouldy at all,' Maisie says. 'It's got a woodburning stove and fairy lights and real, proper beds with quilts and Indian rugs on the floor. And it's only temporary, anyway, while they do the house up. Sheddie explained. It's not like we thought at all, Cookie; you'd like it!'

'I'd hate it!' I growl. 'I can't believe you've fallen for it, Maisie. This wasn't part of the plan!'

'Things change,' she says lightly. 'What are you up to, Cookie?'

❀❀❀❀❀❀❀❀❀❀❀❀❀❀❀❀❀❀❀❀❀

I roll my eyes. 'I'm helping out with the preparations for a big chocolate festival; you'd love it, Maisie.'

'A chocolate festival? Wow. Anyway, are you coming back soon? We're packing everything up and we don't know what to do with your stuff. Mum says if you don't show up soon, she'll call Harry's mum and get Sheddie to drive over there and fetch you.'

'Don't let her do that,' I hiss, alarmed. 'Make up an excuse, anything – just keep her away from Harry or I'm stuffed. I am so, so close to sorting things. I just need another day or so. Stay strong, Maisie!'

'Oh they're coming back with ice creams, better go,' my sister says. 'Bye-eee!'

The phone goes dead, and so does my heart.

It looks like I'm on my own with this. There is still no reply from my so-called dad, so I tap out a second email, keeping it short and to the point.

Hey, Dad,

I can call you that, right? Mr Tanberry just seems too formal. Hope you've had a chance to read my first email. I know it must be a bit of a surprise to hear from me after all this time, but hopefully it's a good surprise, right? I mean, it's not like you didn't know I existed. Hope you find time to email back soon – there's something I really need to ask you, and it's kind of urgent.

Yours faithfully,
Jake Cooke

I send the email and stare at the screen for ages, as if sheer willpower and determination might make an answer appear. Nothing happens.

I can feel the frustration building inside me again, a kind of desperation. I am clearly not cut out for superhero status. Or maybe Cherry is right, and my plan isn't as foolproof as I imagined. I seriously can't believe my little sisters have caved in and fallen for that loser Sheddie, just because of a trip to the zoo, an ice cream and the promise of a cuddly toy tiger.

I can't afford to stay away much longer; the way they're going, they'll be picking out tie-dyed bridesmaids' dresses by the end of the week. It doesn't bear thinking about.

I need a distraction, and it may as well be a useful one; I slouch up to the chocolate workshop, stick my head round the door and tell Paddy I'd like to have a go at putting some kind of stage together.

He takes off his white apron and comes out.

'You're sure about this?' he asks me. 'I'd be very grateful; something simple would be fine, and you can use any of the scrap wood from the storeroom. I can't spare the time myself, or I'd offer to help,'

'I'm happy working on my own,' I tell him.

The storeroom is an old stable, which has been stacked high with packing cases, crates and pallets. Sheets of hardboard, plywood and pine planking lean against one wall, and against another there stands a shelf unit holding saws, tools, jars of nails, brushes and half-used pots of paint.

'OK,' I say. 'I can definitely put something together with all this!'

'Go for it,' Paddy says. 'Don't use anything you're not sure about; no power tools, OK? I don't want your mum chasing me for letting you loose with a chainsaw!'

'I don't need anything fancy,' I promise. 'And I'll be really careful, OK?'

'OK,' Paddy echoes. 'I appreciate the help, Cookie. I

❀❀❀❀❀❀❀❀❀❀❀❀❀❀❀❀❀❀❀❀❀❀❀

wanted to do it myself, but I've had an idea for a new truffle flavour and that has to come first.'

He rakes a hand through his hair, looking like a mad professor.

'You've got to keep it fresh and original,' he says with a shrug. 'Keep those new and unexpected ideas coming. I've tried all kinds in the past: curry truffles, marmalade ones, ones with nutmeg and cinnamon and Earl Grey tea. There was even an experiment with peanut butter and home-grown chillis. I'm not saying they were all saleable, or even edible, but coming up with new ideas is half the fun. I think this new one could be a winner.'

'What is it then?'

'Top secret, for now,' Paddy says. 'I might let you taste test it later on. The TV crew are going to film the whole product-development process tomorrow, so if that goes OK the chances are it could sell well. People will want to buy the truffle they saw being created on TV.'

Paddy heads back to the workshop and I make a start on my project, hauling old pallets and crates down to the flat expanse of grass under the trees where Cherry told me the stage was needed. It's good to have something to do, and a whole afternoon to do it in. I have never made anything on quite such a large scale, but back at the flat I put up shelves and repaired a floorboard and even fixed up a new kitchen counter for Mum, so I am confident I can do this. It's not just a way to pass the time; it's a way to thank the Tanberry-Costello family for making me so welcome.

I start with the basic stage shape that Paddy and Cherry requested, setting out pallets and nailing sheets of hardboard on top. That makes a workable stage, but I add steps made from stacked wooden crates on either side and use pine planks to neaten the front and sides of the stage, and then I give it all a coat of royal blue gloss paint, which looks pretty awesome.

The project takes all afternoon, and I'm not finished yet; I have plans to add a few extra touches, but I need to let the paint dry first. Paddy ambushes me as I am piling the offcuts into a wheelbarrow to take back up to the storeroom.

'Great stuff, Cookie,' he says. 'That's better than anything I had planned!'

I shrug. 'I liked it, sort of switched my brain off for a little bit, and it's done wonders for my suntan. I have a few ideas for finishing it off, but at least you have a stage now!'

'I think you've caught the sun,' Paddy says. 'This is a bit of a heatwave, but the forecast predicts storms for later in the week. I hope they're all gone by Saturday! Anyhow, Cookie, here's a small thank you for the hard labour. Some pocket money while you're here, OK?'

He presses a tenner into my hand, and walks away while I'm still protesting that I don't want it. 'Just take it,' he says over his shoulder. 'Seriously – you've earned it!'

So now I have a suntan and a tenner to add to my £7.92 life savings. The sudden windfall gives me an idea. Maybe if I sent it to Mr Zhao, the cash could buy me some time and act as a down payment until Dad comes through. If Dad comes through.

I know £17.92 is not going to pay for the hole in the restaurant ceiling, but surely it's evidence that I am genuinely sorry. And maybe, by now, Mr Zhao will have calmed down a little and decided against evicting us.

I find a sheet of plain paper in the caravan and start to write:

✿✿✿✿✿✿✿✿✿✿✿✿✿✿✿✿✿✿✿✿✿✿✿✿

Dear Mr Zhao,

I am writing to apologize (again) for the damage caused to your ceiling by our bathtub flood. I want you to know it was a total accident, caused by me dropping noodles on my jeans at work the day before, and our washing machine being broken and not having the cash for the launderette. You cannot blame my little sisters, because even though they left the taps running, I was supposed to be in charge and so if you do want someone to blame, I will step up to the mark.

I am sorry about the lipstick apology. I just wanted to make sure you got the message, but I can see now that a letter would have been better. Sometimes I need to think a bit more before I act, like with the bathtub-washing thing.

I want you to know that I am in the middle of a secret mission to get the money to fix your restaurant ceiling, but things are not going as fast as I had hoped, so I am sending you £17.92 to be going on with. The rest will follow as soon as I can sort it. Don't tell my mum about this, because she will definitely not approve, and I don't want her to know where I am because she will be really upset and worried.

Please reconsider your plan to evict us, because life in a yurt just doesn't bear thinking about.

I honestly didn't mean it.

Yours with regret,
Jake Cooke

Half an hour later, I've cadged an envelope and a first-class stamp from Charlotte, telling her I've written a letter home; I leg it down to the village to catch the post.

15

A letter to Mr Zhao might buy me time, but I need to step things up a little with Greg Tanberry if my plan is going to have any chance of success. Back at the caravan, I fire off another email.

Dear Dad,

I know you are probably weighing up how to answer my emails. I suppose it is hard knowing what to say to the kid you dumped even before he was born, but, trust me, I am not looking for a fight. We have had some very rough times and Mum has struggled to put food on the table, but she is an awesome mum all the same and that more than makes up for you not being there. It's OK, I forgive you – I even have a plan for how you can make up for ignoring us all those years. Put things right a little bit. I think it would ease your conscience a bit, and it would really help me out of a hole. I need you to stop blanking my emails and reply, and then I can tell you more. Please get in touch. Don't worry, it's nothing scary.

Your long-lost son,
Jake Cooke

With every email that fizzes off through the ether to my so-called dad in Australia, my confidence shrinks a little. When I first cooked up this plan, I somehow imagined that Greg Tanberry would jump at the chance of getting to know me and that he'd willingly open his wallet and shell out the money to save my skin. What father wouldn't?

Mine, clearly.

I have never asked him for anything in my whole life, but right now he is my only hope – the only person I know of who has money. Honey says he lives in a posh bungalow in a swish Sydney suburb; he has a swimming pool, a fancy car, designer suits. He could definitely spare a thousand quid to replaster a ceiling and patch a hole in our bathroom floor – let's face it, he probably spends more than that every year on champagne and caviar. He could cut back, downsize a bit to cider and tinned tuna. I think it's the least he could do.

If he would just answer my emails, I know I could persuade him. I could show him that I am not angry or bitter or grasping. I don't want to turn up on his doorstep; I just need a helping hand. I will keep appealing to his better nature, because eventually he might listen.

'Cookie!' Honey's voice rings out through the quiet garden. 'Dinner time!'

Up at the house, we dig into veggie lasagne and salad. Once we've finished eating, Paddy and Charlotte retreat to put in a late shift in the chocolate workshop while the rest of us pitch in to help with preparations for Saturday's festival. Honey spreads paints out across the table, hand-lettering a series of signs; Cherry is writing out menu cards for a chocolate cafe to be sited inside the Indian marquee, which is being delivered on Thursday, and Coco and I are making jam-jar lanterns. Coco does the arty bit, collaging the jam jars with patches of torn tissue paper and silver stars brushed on with thinned white glue. I just put a tea light in each and twist a length of thin wire round the jar necks, bending it up to make a hanging loop.

Skye and Summer are sewing, adjusting the chocolate fairy costumes from the last chocolate festival, adding extra layers of netting and lace and frayed gold taffeta. I can't help thinking that Maisie and Isla would love them.

'Those are really cool,' I comment. 'Like something you'd buy in a shop, only better!'

'Skye's amazing with fabrics and costumes,' Summer tells me. 'She can make something awesome out of a few old scraps. I'm just helping, but Skye's got real talent – a while ago she helped out with the costumes for a TV film that was shot locally. If in doubt, just remember that Skye's the awesome twin!'

'No, Summer is!' Skye argues. 'You should see her dance, Cookie; she's amazing. But her real talents are patience and kindness and enthusiasm – the little kids at the dance school really look up to her. She's a great teacher!'

'You're both fab,' Coco chips in. 'But let's be clear – I am the sister who is going to change the world, OK? I'll be world famous for saving the giant panda or stopping global warming or something.'

'Or something is right,' Honey teases. 'What about you, Cookie? What's your talent? What's your skill?'

❀❀❀❀❀❀❀❀❀❀❀❀❀❀❀❀❀❀❀❀❀

I frown. I am not sure I have a special talent. I like making things and I'm pleased with the way today's makeshift stage has shaped up, but I am not sure that counts, really. I'd like it to; I'd like to be as interesting and talented as my new half-sisters.

'This chocolate festival is going to be hard work,' Coco is saying. 'But should we do something before that? All of us? Show Cookie a bit of the area maybe?'

Honey raises an eyebrow. 'Hey – we totally should,' she says. 'Tomorrow, maybe? Before things get too crazy around here. A bike ride up to the moors? A picnic? There are loads of places you'd like, Cookie – the smugglers' caves, the woods, the weir; it'll be cool.'

Mild panic sets in at the idea of giving up a day to have fun when I know time is so short, but I don't want to seem ungrateful.

'I haven't been to any of those places for ages,' Summer is saying. 'Alfie would be well up for it too.'

'Lawrie will come,' Coco says. 'And Paddy says there are storms coming later in the week, so we should definitely do it tomorrow, before the weather breaks.'

'Cookie?' Honey asks. 'What d'you think?'

❀❀❀❀❀❀❀❀❀❀❀❀❀❀❀❀❀❀❀

'OK,' I say. 'Why not? I haven't got a bike, but maybe I could borrow one?'

'Dad would lend you his, I'm sure,' Cherry cuts in. 'Shay's not working tomorrow, so he can come too. I'll ask him to bring his guitar!'

'Ri-ight,' Honey says, wrinkling her nose a little. 'OK. If you want to. Fine.'

I get the feeling that this is not fine, not by a long way; as if Honey actually wants to exclude Cherry and Shay from the expedition. The others look embarrassed, but Cherry just grins and shrugs and says she'll text Shay, that it'll be fun. It's weird – it's the second or third time I've noticed an edge of awkwardness – frostiness – between Honey and Cherry. I've no idea why, but I'm not stupid; I can tell that Honey doesn't like Cherry, not one bit.

Later, as Coco and I are stacking the finished jam-jar lanterns in the utility room, I ask how come Honey is so snippy with her stepsister, and she looks at me, amazed.

'Nobody told you?' she asks. 'Wow. It's kind of basic; it's why we all walk on eggshells whenever Honey is around. She literally cannot stand Cherry.'

✿✿✿✿✿✿✿✿✿✿✿✿✿✿✿✿✿✿✿✿✿✿✿

I frown. 'OK, but why?'

'Honey had a problem with Paddy and Cherry right from the start,' Coco says. 'She's mellowed, definitely, since she got back from Australia; she's pretty accepting of Paddy now. But it's more complicated with Cherry.'

'How come?'

Coco shakes her head. 'Thing is, three years ago, when Cherry first came to Tanglewood – well, Shay was Honey's boyfriend. He ditched her for Cherry.'

'Ouch!' I comment. 'That's gotta hurt. But three years? Well, that's a long time to hold a grudge.'

'Tell me about it,' she says. 'It's not like Cherry planned it. I mean, you can't help who you fall for, can you? Sometimes, I get the feeling that Honey wants to be friends, but she can't quite let herself move on and forgive. Sucks, right?'

It really does. I'm amazed that a years-old feud is keeping Honey and Cherry apart; both have been awesome to me, making me feel like part of the family, yet they can't reach out to each other. Maybe I can talk to Honey and help her to see how crazy this is?

We head back into the kitchen just as Honey is handing

❁❁❁❁❁❁❁❁❁❁❁❁❁❁❁❁❁❁❁❁❁❁❁❁

out glasses of chocolate milkshake, and then Paddy and Charlotte come in with a tray of sample chocolates.

'OK,' Paddy announces. 'I want you to help me with a taste test, kids. This is the new truffle flavour! I just need to decide between these two variations.'

The box is passed around the kitchen: some of the truffles have a kind of biscuit-crumb crunch worked through the truffle; some are smooth inside with a biscuit-crumb coating. They are all rich and creamy and totally addictive.

'Go easy, Coco,' Honey teases. 'You're practically inhaling them!'

'I am not!' Coco argues. 'They are good, though. What do you think, Cookie?'

'I prefer the ones that are crunchy inside.' Skye says.

'No, the others, definitely,' Summer argues. 'I mean, I wouldn't eat lots of them because they are so rich, but the crunchy on the outside ones are definitely the best!'

Paddy is watching me, waiting for my verdict.

'I think so too,' I say honestly. 'They're both awesome, though!'

✿✿✿✿✿✿✿✿✿✿✿✿✿✿✿✿✿✿✿✿✿

'That version it is then,' Paddy says decisively. 'I think you're right, but I wanted to give you the last call, Cookie. You're the inspiration.'

I frown, confused.

'Dad's created a truffle for all of us sisters,' Cherry explains. 'They're bestsellers now: mine is called Cherry Crush, and there's Marshmallow Skye, Summer's Dream, Coco Caramel, Sweet Honey – all based on our favourite tastes, y'see. So Dad wants to include you, and he's thinking maybe something like Cookie Crumble for the name. What d'you think?'

Suddenly there's a lump in my throat that has nothing to do with chocolate truffles; Paddy, Charlotte and the sisters have made it clear that as far as they are concerned, I am one of the family. I take a deep breath in, feeling a little overwhelmed.

'Nice one,' I say. 'Never had a chocolate named after me before.'

'It's still at the design stage,' Charlotte says. 'We want to add one last element before we're done, but it looks like we're working along the right lines. Glad you like it!'

Honey grins. 'Yeah, I guess this means you're one of us, right?'

I guess maybe it does.

16

The next day, we meet in the village at ten o'clock; the others study maps and argue about routes and I just hitch up my rucksack, push off from the kerb and follow the crowd. It's like being in some kind of mad teenage Famous Five adventure; we cycle through tiny lanes all overgrown with honeysuckle hedges, pedalling single file and wobbling dangerously every time a car zooms past. There are a lot of hills and the day is hot, so progress is slow, but the sky is such a vivid blue and the honeysuckle smell is so heady and sweet that nobody really minds.

There's a rough track that leads through the woods, and most of us have to walk there anyway, except for Shay and Lawrie who have mountain bikes. The old path down to the smugglers' caves is closed and unsafe, so we stop for lunch by a fast-flowing river, which has been dammed to create a weir.

I can't help being reminded of the disaster at The Paper Dragon, but the lure of the cold water is strong, and soon I'm peeling off my T-shirt to wade in and join the others. Back ashore, the twins are spreading out rugs and checked cloths for the picnic. Everybody has brought something, even me (squashed cheese sandwiches, if you want to know) and when it's all laid out it looks amazing. There is cold pizza and salad and sausage rolls, crisps, hard-boiled eggs, hummus and falafel; there are cupcakes with multi-coloured frosting and home-made chocolate brownies and fresh fruit salad; all that and more. Alfie lowers big bottles of Coke and lemonade into the icy water to keep them cool, anchored by lengths of string.

'How long have you been with Alfie?' I ask Summer, helping myself to a sandwich.

'A while,' she says. 'He's OK, y'know. He's stuck by me through some difficult times.'

I glance across to where Skye is loafing in the sun with a book. 'No boyfriend for Skye?' I ask quietly.

Summer shrugs. 'She had a long-distance romance with

a boy called Finch around the time I got together with Alfie. Finch's mum, Nikki, is the producer for the reality TV show – the clipboard lady. Things just fizzled out, I think. They're still friends; we asked Finch up for the Chocolate Festival, but he says he can't make it. Probably for the best . . .'

Alfie flops down beside us, and the conversation switches to light and easy; we eat and drink and laze in the sun. The buzz of chatter goes on around me, but I feel detached somehow, aloof; I want to relax and enjoy it all, but anxiety about what is going on back at home crowds in and ruins everything. Unable to help myself, I sneak away, perching on a rock beside the river at some distance from the others to check my mobile.

Surprise surprise, not a single thing from Dad; there's a text from Mum, though.

Jake, I know you're hiding out at Harry's but we need to talk. I've been calling Harry's flat, but we're moving on Saturday – please come home!

I fire off a hasty reply.

Mum, chill, OK? Everything's cool, I promise – I just need some time out!

And there's a text from Maisie that makes me want to

❀❀❀❀❀❀❀❀❀❀❀❀❀❀❀❀❀❀❀❀❀

chuck my mobile into the weir; I would, if it weren't the only way I have of contacting home and Dad.

Guess what, Cookie? she has written. **Sheddie made us veggie curry last night! It was awesome. I might go veggie too, soon. Today he is teaching us t'ai chi. I think you should give Sheddie a chance, because honestly, Cookie, you would really like him.**

I would *not* like him, I text back. **I may as well just stay in Kitnor, because it looks like you're getting on fine without me.**

I press SEND, drop the mobile into my trainer and wade into the water, then do a fast front crawl right up to the weir itself. I hate Sheddie; I hate that he is there in our flat, creeping around my sisters, doing all the right things, winning them over. For years we've had a shoestring life; we've got by, nothing more. Summer holidays were about the swings in the park and lazy mornings loafing around the flat, about bus trips out to Bethnal Green to sunbathe in Gran's tiny back garden. Now, abruptly, this Sheddie person shows up and suddenly every day's a party, with tourist trips and fancy dinners and new skills to learn. Sheddie has a hundred tiny

150

ways to worm his way into my sisters' hearts, but I don't trust him, not one bit.

I let the ice-cold water pelt my face and shoulders, taking my breath away; the assault beats my anger down to nothing. When I can't stand it any more, I let myself float away from the weir, back into the deepest part of the river. I lie on my back, eyes closed, face to the sky, arms wide; I let the sun warm me again, let the soft drift of the river wash away my frustration.

When finally I am calm enough to wade ashore again, I see Honey sitting on the rocks at the river's edge, arms hooked round her legs, her whole posture hunched, haunted, sad.

'What's up?' I ask, hauling myself on to the bank. 'You look like I feel.'

She picks up her iPhone, scans the screen and sighs heavily.

'Boys,' she tells me. 'You can never trust them. So much for texting me every day!'

'Boyfriend?' I query. 'What's his name again – Ash?'

'That's him,' she tells me. 'He still hasn't been in touch. Days and days without a single call, a single text!'

❀❀❀❀❀❀❀❀❀❀❀❀❀❀❀❀❀❀❀

'Maybe he lost his phone?' I suggest.

She sighs. 'Yeah, right. He was supposed to be going inter-railing through Italy and Spain and France and then maybe coming over to see me here, but he hasn't mentioned that for ages and now he's gone all quiet. I can't help taking it as a sign he's changed his mind. It's a while since we saw each other. I can't blame him if he doesn't feel the same . . .'

'More likely he's just exploring, having fun,' I say, but that doesn't seem to be the right answer either.

'Let's just say I've had a run of bad luck with boys,' Honey says. 'I've a knack for picking out the losers, the ones who hurt me. I got hurt once . . .'

'Was that Shay?' I ask, my voice no more than a whisper.

'Who told you?' she says. 'Well, I don't suppose it matters who; it's not exactly a secret. Everyone knew at the time. It was horrible, Cookie. Felt like everyone was laughing at me, and the worst of it was that I had to share a house with Cherry – can you imagine?'

'Not good,' I say.

'No, not good at all. I went right off the rails. I wanted to lash out, show people I didn't care, but the only person I really hurt was myself. I wasn't about to let it happen again, so I didn't let anyone get too close – and then I met Ash. I thought I could trust him, but it looks like I was wrong.'

I shake my head. 'Honey, this will all work out,' I tell her. 'I bet it's something simple, like a lost phone or a lost charger. Or he's just got sidetracked with exploring and probably hasn't even sussed you're worried.'

'Maybe,' Honey says. 'I don't really think he'd dump me without saying a word. He's better than that, seriously. It just bugs me, when you're waiting for a message that never comes. Speaking of which, has Dad mailed you yet?'

'What do you think?'

'I think not,' Honey says. 'I did try to warn you – he's a bit useless. We really lucked out in the dad department, didn't we?'

'Looks like,' I say. 'At least you've got Paddy, though. He's OK. My Mum has hooked up with this weirdo hippy bloke called Sheddie – he's all dreadlocks and t'ai chi and he's trying to make my little sisters go veggie.'

'Nice,' she says sarcastically. 'Although, actually, maybe – maybe he is? Coco is veggie, y'know. And Mum does t'ai chi. And dreadlocks . . . well, that can be a look. Just sayin'.'

✿✿✿✿✿✿✿✿✿✿✿✿✿✿✿✿✿✿✿✿✿✿

'Not you as well,' I growl. 'My sisters promised to give him the silent treatment, but he's got them eating out of his hand. Ugh.'

'What's wrong with him, exactly?' Honey asks. 'Nicks things? Hits people? Snorts drugs? Leaves the toilet seat up when he's been to the loo?'

'I haven't actually met him,' I admit. 'I don't think he does those things, but who knows? You don't understand!'

'Maybe not,' she says with a shrug. 'I can see why you're upset, but – well, sometimes, when parents split, it's kind of inevitable that some day they are going to get together with someone new. It happened with Mum and Paddy, and it happened with my dad – um, our dad – and Emma. It's just the way life is. You might not like it –'

'I don't!' I argue. 'And this is different. Paddy's not some no-hope hanger-on without a penny to his name.'

'Actually, he kind of was,' Honey remarks. 'I thought so to start with, anyway. But he's turned out to be pretty OK; I admit I might have got things a little bit wrong. Maybe this is different, Cookie, but all I am saying is give the bloke a chance; he might be OK. After all, your mum clearly likes him.'

❀❀❀❀❀❀❀❀❀❀❀❀❀❀❀❀❀❀❀❀❀

'Yeah. Well, she has pretty dismal taste in men, my dad, for one.'

'Our dad,' she corrects me. 'Yeah, can't really argue with that one. Just – well, try giving him a chance. You might be surprised.'

'Will you ever give Cherry a chance?' I counter.

Honey shuts down instantly, her empathy and easy charm gone. Her mouth is a hard line, her eyes cold.

'Never gonna happen, Cookie,' she says, and walks back to the others.

17

The next day, my legs ache from cycling and my shoulders are burnt and peeling from where I sat too long with my T-shirt off and forgot to keep applying suncream. It was an awesome day; after the weir we freewheeled downhill and climbed over rocks and crags to reach the smugglers' caves, which were majorly spooky and impressive. On the way home, we saw a herd of Exmoor ponies on the moor and stopped off for chips and cans of pop in a touristy village not far from Kitnor.

If my little sisters are getting a holiday in London, then I am definitely getting one here; but I am making zero progress in getting my dad to communicate. It's a pity I can't get myself over to Sydney, Australia, and turn up on his doorstep, because I think he might have a tougher job ignoring me then. Although he has ignored me my whole life, so maybe not.

Dear Dad-I've-Never-Met,

I am trying to stay hopeful. I am telling myself that my emails to you are going into a spam folder or something; I am telling myself that you are not actually blanking me. You wouldn't do that, right? You are my dad, flesh and blood, and although we have never met there is still a link between us that neither one of us can change. You might not want to be my dad, but you are. I might not want to be your son, but I am. We are both stuck with it.

The only other thing I can think of is that you don't believe me. Maybe you think I am an imposter, a scammer, a conman. If that is the case, then I will attach some evidence that might convince you: a photo of me, taken yesterday. I may be squinting a little bit because it was very sunny, but I think you will see that I look very like you all the same. At least, I look very like you in the old pictures I have seen. You are probably a bit different now.

I am not trying to con you, I promise, but I do need your help. If you have a heart, please reply and I will explain.

Yours in desperation,
Jake Cooke

I ignore the new day's batch of texts and voicemails from Mum and snarl over a text from Maisie that tells me Sheddie is taking them swimming today.

Instead of brooding, I decide to finish the festival stage. I drag a whole heap of driftwood branches from the beach up the rickety cliff steps and fix two of them in the back corners to hold a backdrop – I haven't quite worked that bit out yet, but I know I want this to look like a real stage and not some handmade effort. I want it to be cool. The remaining branches I build into a crazy twiggy archway that curves over the front of the stage to frame the performers; it takes forever to construct, but it looks amazing.

It's hot work; the heatwave seems to have ramped up a notch today, and even the air feels sticky and oppressive. As the morning wears on, some of the sisters appear to check out what's going on.

'Pretty cool,' Summer says, surveying the work in progress. 'It looks amazing, but the arch would be even better all draped with fairy lights.'

'I know where there's a spare lot,' Coco offers.

'Awesome,' I say. 'I'm going to make some kind of backdrop, but I'm not sure if it should be hardboard or something else.'

'What about a painted sheet?' Skye suggests. 'We could paint it and drape it between the branches. There are a whole load of old sheets in the attic, if you want one.'

Half an hour later, the four of us are working together. Coco brings a wheelbarrow of half-used paint pots and mismatched brushes from the stable storeroom; she starts painting stars and crescent moons on the royal blue background of the stage sides while I paint spiralling ivy tendrils on the tall branches at the back of the stage.

'You're arty as well as practical,' Skye comments approvingly, looking up from the white cotton sheet she has spread across the grass. Summer is neatly painting a big curving rainbow on this while Skye maps out the words *Tanglewood Chocolate Festival* in curly, quirky letters. It looks amazing, especially once we've filled in the letters with black paint

❀❀❀❀❀❀❀❀❀❀❀❀❀❀❀❀❀❀❀❀❀

and tacked the backdrop in place. Working with the sisters is fun and makes me feel like a proper part of the family; it's a good feeling.

Draping the fairy lights across the arch is the final touch, and I balance on a stepladder and stretch over to make sure everything is as perfect as it can be.

'Mum and Paddy will *love* this,' Summer tells me. 'It looks amazing!'

'Way better than anything Paddy had planned,' Skye agrees. 'It's a piece of art!'

Coco frowns and wrinkles her nose. 'What if it rains, though?' she asks. 'There are supposed to be storms later, right? The fairy lights will get wet and then they won't work. Should we cover everything in tarpaulin? There are a few big sheets of plastic down in the storeroom.'

'It's too hot for a storm,' I argue. 'Stifling, really —'

'That's exactly how it feels when a storm is brewing,' Skye tells me. 'Sort of sticky and oppressive. Coco could be right.'

So in the end we hide the finished stage under draped tarpaulins, and I like the idea because I want to see the look on Paddy's face when it's unveiled.

After that, the sisters drift back up to the house to help with the baking for Saturday's chocolate cafe. I help in the chocolate workshop with Paddy and Cherry for a while, apron on, my hair held back by a spotted bandana, pirate style. Paddy is working long hours now to produce enough chocolate stock and to showcase the new flavours he's been working on; he shows me a new machine he has invested in, a kind of electrical engraving needle that allows you to inscribe even the tiniest words or delicate patterns into chocolate.

'We're making chocolate fortunes for the festival,' Cherry explains. 'Want to have a try?'

It turns out that I'm too clumsy to write or draw anything very useful with the engraver, but Cherry is neat and steady, using a magnifying glass, and Paddy goes off to fetch a tray of tiny moulded heart discs for her to work on. I write out a list of fortune words, the kind of thing you mind find on a Love Heart sweet. It's harder than you think. 'Smile', 'hug me', 'stay strong', 'be kind', 'make someone laugh', 'share', 'be brave', 'chill' and 'believe in magic' all make the cut; 'always answer emails', 'never wash your jeans in the bath' and 'beware of falling ceilings' do not. I guess that's fair enough.

As we're working, Honey barges in, her smile a mile wide,

❀❀❀❀❀❀❀❀❀❀❀❀❀❀❀❀❀❀❀❀❀❀

yesterday's coolness forgotten. Honey may have a short fuse but she doesn't hold a grudge for long – except with Cherry, that is.

'Quick, Cookie!' she says. 'I've just invented something totally amazing and I want you to taste it for me. I think it would be perfect for the festival. Come and see, and tell me what you think; am I a genius, or am I a genius?'

We head across to the house, which is just as busy as the chocolate workshop. In the conservatory, Sandy, Lawrie and Coco are folding printed card into little boxes ready to be filled with chocolates on Saturday; in the kitchen, Charlotte and the twins are mixing up enough chocolate fridge cake to feed a small army.

Honey's invention stands at the end of the kitchen table – a tall glass of layered milkshake with a strawberry skewered on the edge of the rim; enough to make anyone's mouth water.

'Taste it,' she says, handing the glass to me. 'Tell me what you think. I might call it a strawberry chocolate cream smoothie. Or should I call it a milkshake? Or a frappé? What sounds better?'

'Milkshake,' Summer says.

❀❀❀❀❀❀❀❀❀❀❀❀❀❀❀❀❀❀

'Smoothie,' Charlotte argues. 'It's great, though, whatever you call it!'

I take a sip of the drink. It's smashed-up strawberries at the bottom, then a layer of milk chocolate shake, then one of dark, with a topping of cream and grated chocolate. It tastes awesome.

'Don't care what you call it,' I tell her. 'It's amazing!'

Honey glows with pride. 'I knew you'd like it!' she says. 'Paddy? What do you think? Too heavy on the dark chocolate? Just right? I spent ages trying to do a peanut butter and banana layer, but the mushed-up strawberries work loads better – and everyone likes strawberries, right?'

Paddy takes a sip of the concoction and nods his approval. 'Spot on, just the right balance. I'll have to get you designing and inventing in the chocolate workshop, Honey!'

'Thanks, Paddy,' she says.

Cherry takes a sip and gives her stepsister the thumbs up too. 'Cookie's right, it's out of this world!'

Honey smiles sweetly at this, then turns her back on Paddy, Charlotte and Summer. 'Like I care what you think,' she says to Cherry under her breath.

It's so quick, so quiet that I almost miss it – but I don't

miss it, and the spite takes my breath away. Cherry sighs and withdraws quietly, heading back to the chocolate work-shop; the others, oblivious to Honey's barbed comment, decide to take a tea break.

'What?' Honey mouths at me. 'Just being honest!'

I shake my head, unable to meet Honey's eye, but she shrugs and smiles like she doesn't care at all, and I decide to head back to the workshop too.

'What's the big deal?' she hisses, following me outside and tugging at my elbow. 'I never said I was a nice person, did I? I'm not, Cookie, but I'm honest, at least. I don't like her and I don't understand what you see in her.'

'I see someone like us, Honey,' I snap. 'Someone who needs a family, needs to belong. How come you can't see it?'

'She doesn't belong here,' Honey argues. 'She wormed her way in, took everything she wanted from right under our noses – and she fooled everyone. She's fooled you too!'

I break away from Honey's grip.

'You fooled me,' I say harshly. 'I thought you were better than this.'

This time, I'm the one to walk away.

*

'How come you don't react?' I ask Cherry, later, up by the gypsy caravan. 'How come you let her treat you like dirt?'

Cherry shrugs. 'She has her reasons,' she says. 'What can I say? I hurt her – I didn't mean to, but I did. She doesn't like me. I'm kind of used to it now.'

'Doesn't it upset you?'

Cherry blinks. 'Of course it does. It's not always this bad. I think she's hurt that we're friends – a bit jealous maybe.'

'What, just because we talk sometimes?' I ask, incredulous.

'I think so,' Cherry says with a sigh. 'The thing about Honey is . . . she's not as tough as she makes out, not by a long way.'

'I'd noticed.'

'I understand, in a funny way,' Cherry says. 'I wish she didn't feel like that, but I try not to let it get to me. I just keep hoping that some day she'll give me a chance.'

I think about that long after Cherry has gone: chances given, chances not given, chances taken, chances lost. How are you supposed to know which to give, which not?

Mr Zhao
The Paper Dragon
11 Macclesfield St
CHINATOWN London
W1D 4RR

18

I'm in bed by ten, my arms and legs still aching from yesterday's cycle expedition and my stage-building exertions, but I can't sleep; the night is too hot, too sticky to breathe. I push back the patchwork quilt and wrap myself in a sheet instead, but the caravan feels like a sauna. Abruptly, my mobile begins to buzz. Groaning, I pick it up and see that the call is from Maisie. I scramble to sit upright in the caravan bunk.

'Hey, Maisie,' I say. 'Everything OK?'

But on the other end of the phone my little sister is crying. 'Oh, Cookie, it's all gone wrong. Mum knows you're not at Harry's. Or Mitch's. She knows you've run away!'

'How?' I ask, my heart thumping. 'What happened?

Don't cry, Maisie – shhh. And calm down. Someone will hear you!'

'I'm on the top bunk,' Maisie snuffles. 'It makes me feel close to you, now you're not here any more. Isla's asleep and I'm hiding under the duvet with the bedroom door shut. Nobody can hear me.'

Slowly, Maisie's sobbing subsides and I hear her blowing her nose, snuffling slightly.

'It wasn't me that told,' she says at last, her voice steadier now. 'I didn't, I promise.'

'Just tell me, Maisie. What happened?'

There's a big intake of breath at the other end of the line, and my little sister starts to speak. 'Mr Zhao came up to see Mum this evening. He had a letter, and he was showing it to Mum. He gave her some money from out of the envelope and Mum started crying – I don't get it, Cookie, but Mum was really upset and Mr Zhao was all sad too, saying he was sorry you'd got the wrong end of the stick and of course he would never evict us. He couldn't understand why you would think such a thing. What does evict mean?'

'Throw people out of their flat,' I say numbly. 'But I

heard him say it. At least, I think I did! And he was so angry!'

'I don't think he's angry any more,' Maisie says.

If anyone is angry now, I think it's me. I've blown it all, with a stupid letter that was meant to buy me time. Instead, it's ruined everything. I didn't imagine Mr Zhao would show the letter to Mum. I didn't think they were even speaking any more.

'What happened then?' I ask.

'Well, Mum said that she was leaving anyway, that she was sorry to let Mr Zhao down at such a difficult time, but that we were going to Millford. She introduced Mr Zhao to Sheddie and they shook hands and Sheddie said he'd be happy to help with any repairs that might be going on, even though he wasn't a proper carpenter or anything. But I think he could do it, Cookie. He can do all kinds of things.'

'Shut up about Sheddie!' I growl. 'Then what?'

Maisie sighs. 'After Mr Zhao had gone, Mum called Harry again. Harry's mum answered and said she hadn't seen you for a week or so; so then she called Mitch, and he tried to say you were there, but his dad came on the line

❀❀❀❀❀❀❀❀❀❀❀❀❀❀❀❀❀❀

and said you weren't, and that they hadn't seen you for ages. And Sheddie said we should call the police, but Mum got really upset then and said that they couldn't, that if they did the social workers would say she was a bad mother and take you into care.'

'She's not a bad mother!' I protest. 'She's brilliant!'

'I know that,' Maisie says. 'But she is really, really sad and worried, and I am in trouble because I tried to cover for you and everything has gone all wrong. You have to come home now, Cookie, you really do. They're in there now, looking at a map of Somerset because the letter you sent to Mr Zhao had a Somerset postmark.'

Abruptly, Maisie yelps and starts to cry again, and Mum's voice comes on the line.

'Jake? Jake, is that you? Just tell me where you are, love, please. I'm not cross, I'm not angry. I just need to know you're safe!'

'I'm safe,' I say, my voice no more than a whisper. 'Don't worry about me, Mum. I'm trying to sort something out, something important, but I'll be home really soon – I promise.'

'Jake –'

❀❀❀❀❀❀❀❀❀❀❀❀❀❀❀❀❀❀❀❀❀❀

I press the button to end the call, my heart thumping. I feel sick, shaken.

Time is running out. I've been seduced by Tanglewood, sidetracked by my sisters, distracted by new friendships and bike rides and beaches. I ran away and found a different life, and I liked it way too much, and forgot why I was here.

It feels strangely lonely to know that I can't contact Maisie any more. I'm not stupid. I know that any communication with her will be intercepted by Mum from now on, and it's my own fault. I spot a couple of texts from Harry and Mitch, saying they're sorry they couldn't cover for me any longer; but of course there is no email from Dad.

The hurt of it curls inside me like a virus, seeping through my body, making my heart ache. Even if I did turn up on his doorstep in Sydney, he'd probably slam the door in my face. I've been so patient, so polite; but the truth is, he just doesn't care.

Dear Dad,

Well, it's kind of a joke to call you that, but I am not sure what else to call you, so hey.

I know you won't reply to this – why would you? You

❀❀❀❀❀❀❀❀❀❀❀❀❀❀❀❀❀❀❀❀

don't want to face up to your mistakes. You don't want to admit you have a son at all, because that would mean admitting you're a cheat and liar, right? That you had a whole string of affairs and didn't bother to face the consequences. You can't admit I exist because that would be just plain embarrassing – after all, I was raised in a series of scaffy flats and rented houses, and I might be a little bit too rough around the edges to fit into your world.

You know what? I have never asked you for anything in my life. Not your name, not your love, not one single thing. And then something bad happened and I didn't know where to turn, and I thought of you. I thought maybe you could make up for all those years of not being around, and actually help me. I thought it might be something you'd be glad to do.

More fool me.

I think sometimes it is easier not to have a dad at all than to have one who is so spectacularly rubbish.

I won't be bothering you again.

Jake Cooke

❀❀❀❀❀❀❀❀❀❀❀❀❀❀❀❀❀❀❀❀❀❀❀

I press SEND, and almost at once I am consumed by guilt. Why do I do it? Over and over, I act without thinking, get angry, get smart. It makes me feel better, for all of about five minutes – and then sense kicks in and I suss that I've actually made the whole situation worse.

I head up to the house and into the kitchen; Cherry is fixing herself a glass of orange juice from the fridge. 'It's so hot,' she complains. 'I – Cookie, what's wrong? You look awful!'

I sigh. 'Mum knows I've run away and Sheddie wants her to go to the police; my little sister just rang me crying, terrified the police would come after me and take me into care. Let's face it, Dad is never going to answer my emails. The whole plan was rubbish, right from the start. If he was a good guy, he'd have stuck around in the first place, wouldn't he?'

'Maybe you're just making it too easy for him,' Cherry says. 'I mean . . . emails . . . they're very polite and easy to ignore, aren't they?'

'The one I've just sent wasn't,' I admit.

Cherry laughs. 'Good! Maybe it'll rattle him; make him see he can't just keep quiet and hope you'll go away. Don't give up, Cookie – this isn't just about getting the money for the repairs, is it? It's about you making contact with Greg and him acknowledging you. Why not call him? Or Skype?'

'Wouldn't know where to start,' I say. 'If I rang, he'd just hang up.'

'Skype then,' Cherry says. 'There has to be a way of doing it so that he'll listen to you. What have you said in your emails so far? Does he know you're here, with us?'

I frown. 'No, I wanted to do this on my own. Big fail on that one, obviously.'

'Maybe,' she says. 'Doing things solo is all very well, but it's when you work together you really start to make a difference. Teamwork, yeah? But it's good he doesn't know you're here – it does still leave us with the element of surprise. If we can get one of the others to Skype Greg – well, he'd have to take the call, wouldn't he? And then you can take over. I bet Skye or Summer would do it, or Coco. But –'

'But what?'

'Well, Honey's the one to ask, really. She knows Greg better than anyone; she's lived with him. We can ask her to call – that'll do it. And if that doesn't sort things out, then we'll pool our cash and get you a ticket back to London first thing tomorrow. OK?'

'OK,' I say.

For the first time in a week, real hope begins to unfurl inside me.

19

I am holed up in the turret room with Honey Tanberry at half one in the morning, sitting on the window seat, eating Jaffa Cakes and plotting. 'You should have come to me in the first place,' she says. 'I'd have Skyped Dad days ago, and all this would have been sorted.'

She tips her head on one side and looks at me searchingly. 'Plus – I thought we understood each other, Cookie? I thought we were mates. So how come you confided in Cherry, not me?'

'She understood,' I say simply, and Honey scowls.

'She has to have everything,' my half-sister explains. 'My life, my boyfriend, my sisters, my mum – all of it. And now my brother too.'

I roll my eyes. 'That's rubbish and you know it,' I argue.

❀❀❀❀❀❀❀❀❀❀❀❀❀❀❀❀❀❀❀❀❀❀❀

'Your life is better than it's ever been, you told me so yourself. You're at sixth-form college, your AS grades were good and your art teacher wants you to apply for degree courses. Maybe Shay and Cherry fell for each other, but that should be ancient history now. You told me Ash was the only boy you'd ever really cared about.'

'Pity he doesn't feel the same,' Honey sulks. 'Still no texts.'

'He'll be in touch,' I say. 'So, yeah, your mum and your sisters think you're awesome and I do too, but I do not get why you're so mean to your stepsister. It was her idea to ask you to get in touch with Greg – with Dad. And she didn't tell on you when she found out about the fake phone chat you had with Paddy. She could have easily.'

Honey shrugs. 'More fool her.'

I sigh. 'It's like kicking a kitten, Honey. I didn't think you were that kind of person.'

She shrugs again. 'What can I say? I have a mean streak.'

'And I have a big mouth. You told me to get over it.'

'I'm full of good advice,' she quips. 'I just don't like taking it. Don't pick on me, little brother. I've messaged Dad for you, haven't I? We have a plan. He's expecting us to call at one p.m. Sydney time, which is two a.m. here. Not ideal, I

176

admit, but he has his lunch break then, so he should be able to take five minutes; and we don't want an audience, obviously, especially if we're using Mum's computer downstairs.'

Honey no longer has a laptop of her own; her old one had an accident with a swimming pool in Australia, and because of all the cyberbullying stuff that happened while she was there, it was never replaced. Honey went off laptops and social networking overnight.

She doesn't seem to be missing it; her bedroom is an Aladdin's cave of artwork in progress. Self-portraits of a sad-eyed girl gaze out from a series of drawing boards and canvases: an image painted from a shattered mirror, a face hidden behind layers of gauzy fabric, a portrait painted carefully on to an old jigsaw puzzle, with some pieces missing. They are amazing, and they show a very different side of Honey. Underneath the confident drama queen exterior, there is still a lot of hurt.

'Maybe you'll be famous, one day,' I say. 'My big sister, the next Van Gogh. Only with both ears intact, obviously.'

'I'm going to try,' she says. 'Sometimes I think that art's the only thing that matters – it takes all the broken bits of you and makes something good from them, y'know?'

❀❀❀❀❀❀❀❀❀❀❀❀❀❀❀❀❀❀❀❀

I don't know, but I can see that art is a kind of magic for Honey. And OK, I am not an expert, but even I can see that Honey is good, very good. In my imagination I fast-forward a few years, picture the two of us meeting in a cool cafe in London, Honey with an art portfolio under her arm, me – well, I cannot quite envisage me, but I'll be there. I'll be OK.

'It's so *hot*,' Honey complains. 'Sticky-hot. Paddy says there'll be a storm.'

'Nah, it's a heatwave,' I say. 'Can't possibly rain.'

I press my nose against the leaded glass of the window, looking up at the sky; for the first time since I've been at Tanglewood there are no stars, no crescent moon hanging in the velvet dark.

There's a quiet tapping at the door, and Cherry's head appears. 'It's almost two,' she says. 'Shall we go down?'

Honey rolls her eyes. 'Cherry, it's good of you to be so supportive of Cookie,' she says. 'But we don't actually need you for the Skype call. We've got it covered.'

'We'll do it together,' I say, and Honey rolls her eyes.

The three of us are on the landing when the door of the twins' room opens and Skye appears. 'What's going on?'

she whispers. 'We were just going down to grab a couple of drinks and we could hear talking.'

'Nothing's going on,' Cherry says.

'Obviously,' I add. 'No way.'

'So where are you going?' Summer wants to know, peering over Skye's shoulder.

'Nowhere!' Honey says huffily. 'Oh, for goodness' sake! Can't anyone get a little peace and privacy in this house? We're going to Skype Dad, and introduce him to Cookie.'

'Ooh, can we come?' Skye wants to know. 'It should be a family thing, right? Please?'

'Just don't wake up Mum and Paddy,' Honey sighs. 'Cookie needs a bit of privacy here!'

Yet another door creaks open, and Coco peeps out, dressed in an outsize save-the-panda T-shirt. 'I can't sleep,' she says. 'It's *sooo* hot and clammy. I feel like I'm being boiled alive! So why are we all hanging around on the landing in the middle of the night?'

'You tell me,' Honey says, exasperated. 'Right, change of plan, Cookie. We'll do a group Skype. C'mon, you lot – and be *quiet*!'

We creep down the stairs, hardly daring to breathe as

we cross the lower landing where Paddy and Charlotte's bedroom is. Once we're downstairs, the sisters crowd into the shadowy kitchen and pour glasses of cold orange juice from the fridge, which cools everyone down a little. Fred the dog attaches himself to the gang, whimpering a little. 'I actually think there is going to be thunder,' Coco says, stroking his fur. 'Fred always seems to know. He hates it. Bet you anything. Paddy said there'd be a storm.'

We trek through to Charlotte's computer, which is on a desk cluttered with invoices, orders and Chocolate Box paperwork at the back of the conservatory. Honey sits down on the swivel chair just as the first flash of lightning crackles across the sky outside.

'Wow,' Summer says, stepping a little closer to her twin. 'That's impressive.'

Her words are drowned out by a crash of thunder so loud it seems to shake the windows. The rain starts to fall, lashing against the glass, streaming down in rivulets. It feels a bit like the end of the world, and Fred the dog presses his head against my hand, and I stroke him, trying to soothe his whimpers.

'Perfect night for a Skype call,' Honey says, logging into

❀❀❀❀❀❀❀❀❀❀❀❀❀❀❀❀❀❀❀❀❀❀

the computer and pulling up the Skype icon. 'Never let anyone say it's dull here at Tanglewood. Now look, back off, people, just for a minute. Let's not swamp Dad, OK? We're going to hit him with a major shock here; let's go gently. And let's hope he remembered we're calling.'

We step back, out of view of the webcam, and Honey clicks on CALL. After a few rings, the call connects and a picture fills the screen: my so-called dad. He's a good-looking, fair-haired man in a shirt and tie; his sleeves are rolled up, but he manages to look groomed, confident, comfortable. The chunky silver watch on his wrist probably cost more than Mum earns in a whole year. Or possibly two.

He doesn't look like he could be my dad, not in a million years. He looks too polished, too slick, too charming. Disappointment floods through me, colder than the rain sliding down the windowpanes.

'How's my favourite girl?' he says to Honey, and that is obviously the wrong thing to say, because Skye, Summer and Coco are mock-outraged, crowding in around their sister to argue with Greg Tanberry about which one is his favourite. I watch him charm his way out of the gaffe with easy skill, asking Honey how her painting is going, asking Summer about her dancing, Skye what decade is inspiring her fashion sense at the moment, Coco about her pony and her wildlife campaigns. He reels them in, keeps them smiling, mesmerized by the screen, and when Skye pulls Cherry into the circle he is lovely to her too, although she's clearly the outsider; he doesn't have much of a clue about what makes her tick.

'I'm honoured to be sharing a middle-of-the-night thunderstorm with you,' he says, as lightning flashes again and thunder follows fast on its tail. 'Can't say I'm missing that fabulous British weather, though! I think you'd better be getting back to bed now, girls; what would your mum say?'

'We're going,' Honey promises. 'In a minute. But the reason we called – look, Dad, this is kind of massive. I can't tell you how we found out – what happened – it's complicated. But the thing is, we found out that we have a half-brother, and we've tracked him down, and – well, he's here.'

Watching from the sidelines, I see Greg Tanberry's face struggle to stay bright and cheerful; behind the hearty smile I notice irritation, anger, fear.

'What half-brother?' he asks, but there's a kind of defeat in his voice. He knows there is no escape.

Honey gets up from the swivel chair and pulls me forward,

sits me down. I see my face appear in the small side window, watch Greg Tanberry's face as it registers shock, surprise and, finally, a kind of fascination.

'Go on!' Honey says. 'Talk to him, Cookie!'

My mouth feels dry as dust and my heart hammers so hard it feels loud as the thunderclaps.

'Dad?' I say a little shakily. 'I'm Jake. Jake Cooke.'

20

I half expect him to yell and rage and cut the call dead. I half believe he will deny all knowledge of me, tell me I'm a liar, tell me I'm nobody at all, but that doesn't happen.

'Jake?' he asks gently. 'Is it really you?'

I find that I cannot speak, that my voice is full of hurt and love and loss, and there is no room left for words. Instead I nod and smile and try very hard not to cry, and although it seems ridiculous I stretch out my hand and touch the computer screen. I think if I could touch him, touch this man who is my dad but has never been a dad to me, then I could make him understand everything that's in my heart, make him understand how much I have missed him. Has he missed me?

'I emailed,' I say, my voice wobbly. 'You didn't answer.'

'I thought it was some kind of scam,' he says. 'I didn't realize.'

'It wasn't a scam,' I tell him. 'It was just me. I came here to find you – to find my sisters. I didn't know that they existed, but I knew about you; I think I've been looking for you for a long time.'

I think I have, although I didn't really know it. In my hopes, in my dreams, in my saddest moments – those were the times I needed a dad, an anchor. And now, with life turning upside down all around me, I need him more than ever.

'I'm in trouble,' I say. 'I ran away to find you, to ask for help; there was an accident, and it was my fault, and we're losing the flat because of it. Everything's gone wrong. I need some money. I mean, I can pay it back some day, maybe, but I need it fast and I thought that you could help me, because you're my dad and I know you'd *want* to help me, if you could. I don't know the exact amount, but maybe eight or nine hundred quid should do it, and it would totally save our lives.'

Dad's face goes very still. I can see him closing down, like pulling down the shutters on a shop, locking the door.

❁❁❁❁❁❁❁❁❁❁❁❁❁❁❁❁❁❁❁❁❁❁❁

'You're asking me for money?' he says, incredulous. 'Seriously? Fourteen years and you track me down from the other side of the world to ask me for *money*? Is this a joke?'

'It's not a joke!' I protest. 'Mum's lost her job and the landlord threatened to put us out on the street, and it's all my fault.'

Greg Tanberry starts to laugh. 'You know what, Jake Cooke?' he says. 'You're quite something. You are just like your mother. That was all Alison wanted too – money. Money to look after the baby, money for rent, money for clothes, money for food; she thought she'd found a meal ticket for life. She trapped me, set me up because she thought she'd have a cushy life, with some idiot on hand to pay all the bills. She was a gold-digger, Jake. Well, I guess the apple never falls far from the tree.'

A wave of anger rushes through me, so powerful it just about lifts me off my feet.

'*Shut up!*' I yell, and my fist thumps down on the table and scatters papers everywhere. 'You're a liar! A *liar*!'

I can't see the screen any more because my eyes are blinded by tears, but I know I need to get away. I'm on my

✿✿✿✿✿✿✿✿✿✿✿✿✿✿✿✿✿✿✿✿✿✿✿

feet, pushing past my half-sisters, shoving open the French windows and stepping into the storm.

'Cookie!' Honey is yelling. 'Hang on, just ignore him – he's an idiot.'

'Jake, wait up! Come back!'

It barely registers. I'm outside, already drenched in the rain, running away from the house, away from the humiliation. Fourteen years it took me to find my dad; two minutes to lose him forever. He's vile and mean and greedy and cruel. I would rather spend my whole life without a father than settle for one so shoddy.

Rain runs down my face like tears, soaks my clothes and jabs my skin like ice-cold needles. My hair is plastered to my head. I'm no longer hot now, but freezing, shivering, teeth chattering.

'Cookie! Wait!'

Behind me Honey, Cherry and the others are following, but I cannot face them now; I don't know if I can ever face them again.

Lightning tears across the sky, a jagged stab of electricity lighting up the trees. I run beneath the branches as the thunder crashes above me, shove past the carefully

❀❀❀❀❀❀❀❀❀❀❀❀❀❀❀❀❀❀❀❀❀❀❀

crafted stage all wrapped in tarpaulins, run down across the wet grass, pull open the rickety gate and stumble on to the cliff steps, slippery with rain. I pick my way down, hanging on to the wobbly railing, glad that my trainers have good grip.

At last my feet sink into soft sand. I can see the ocean, a vast curve of velvet black glinting in the light of a slender moon. The clouds are parting, wiping away anger, damping down the storm, and the rain is softer now, less punishing.

'Cookie!'

I look back to see Honey and Cherry making their way down the cliff steps, and my heart lurches as an ear-piercing scream rips through the night, followed by a clattering, scrambling sound. Someone has fallen.

'Cherry!' Honey's voice yells out. 'Cherry, hang on! Help! Somebody, help!'

Fred the dog is barking, a terrible, anguished bark that goes on and on, and I'm running back again, scrabbling my way up the steps to where Honey is lying across the uneven steps, stretching down to hold her stepsister's hands. I can see Cherry's face, a pale oval of terror in the darkness, her breath coming in ragged gasps.

'I'll get Mum and Paddy!' Summer yells from above us, turning back into the garden. Skye throws herself down next to Honey, hanging on to her waist.

'I can't hold her, Cookie,' Honey says. 'Do something!'

I can't get near enough to Cherry from the steps so I run back down again and work my way across the jagged rock face in the darkness, trying to edge myself upwards. I'm vaguely aware of Coco behind me, telling me to go slowly, to watch out for gorse on the rock face, to hang on and pull myself up. I can see the pale blur of Cherry's T-shirt in the darkness, and feel the rock, wet and precarious, beneath my feet.

'Don't fall, Cherry,' I hear Honey shout through the rain. 'Hang on, please hang on. I'm sorry for all the bad stuff I've said and done. I'm sorry, so sorry! Hang on, please!'

It seems to take forever, but it's actually less than a minute before I reach Cherry. I steady myself, wedging myself against the root of a stunted tree that's growing out of the cliff a couple of metres below her. In that moment there's another lightning flash and I see Cherry clearly, her feet flailing over wet rock, finding a foothold and losing it again,

189

❀❀❀❀❀❀❀❀❀❀❀❀❀❀❀❀❀❀❀❀❀❀

Honey's hands digging into her wrists. As darkness swallows the light again, I stretch out to grab her waist.

'Let go!' I yell to Honey, and Cherry falls back against me, and we slip a little and land roughly against the gnarled old tree.

In the end, I hold Cherry's arm and help her climb down to where Coco is waiting at the foot of the cliff.

By the time Paddy, Charlotte and Summer arrive, we're sitting on the wet sand, clinging on to each other, Honey and Cherry and me, with Skye and Coco huddled beside us.

'I'm sorry, I'm so, so sorry,' Honey keeps whispering, and Cherry just nods and shivers and rests her head against Honey's shoulder and says thank you over and over again. I stretch my arms round them both and wait for my heartbeat to slow again, wait for the fear and adrenalin and elation to fade.

Just half an hour ago I thought I'd lost everything. Now I know that I have gained far more than I've lost; one jigsaw piece is gone forever, but a whole bunch more I never knew I needed are there in its place. I can make a picture after all.

❀❀❀❀❀❀❀❀❀❀❀❀❀❀❀❀❀❀❀❀❀❀❀

There are more tears, more hugs, anguished explanations. I wait for Paddy and Charlotte to get angry, get mad, but they don't do that; they just hug us each in turn, me included, and help us climb back up the cliff steps, slowly, steadily, by torchlight.

And then we're all walking back across the grass, and the rain has finally stopped and the clouds clear, and the crescent moon shines down on all of us. The others get up to the house first, head in through the kitchen door. Honey and Cherry and I follow last of all, arms round each other, Fred the dog running on ahead.

We're walking through the cherry trees when a ramshackle van turns in through the gates, crunching across the gravel, headlights sweeping over us.

'Who the heck?' I mutter, and Honey and Cherry shake their heads, baffled.

Paddy and Charlotte reappear in the doorway, frowning. Nobody turns up to visit at three in the morning, do they?

The van shudders to a halt and the doors slide open. A woman carrying a little girl wrapped in a blanket steps down on the gravel, another child, older, leaning into her sleepily. On the other side of the van, a man appears; a tall, wiry man with long dreadlocks pulled back into a pony-tail. Suddenly I feel sick, scared, horrified.

Sheddie.

'Jake,' Mum says, her face breaking into a weary grin. 'Oh, Jake, thank God we've found you!'

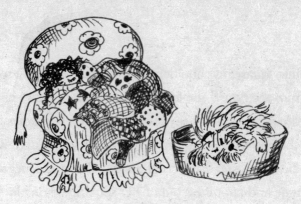

21

Mum puts Isla down and my littlest sister rubs her eyes and squints up at me through the darkness. 'There he is!' she cries, and she and Maisie tumble across the grass towards me, hair fluttering out behind them. I can't run, I can't hide. I stretch out my arms and gather them in, hugging them close, laughing in spite of myself, inhaling the scent of cheap shampoo and bubblegum and home.

'You're wet, Cookie,' Isla declares, unimpressed. 'All soggy! Yuck!'

'Mum got my mobile,' Maisie is saying, breathless, tearful. 'She checked back through my texts and worked out where you were. I'm sorry, Cookie!'

'It's OK,' I whisper. 'It's OK, I promise.'

Above her head I see Mum coming towards me and I tilt

my chin, square my shoulders. In the thin yellow light spilling out from the house, she looks older somehow, blue shadows beneath her eyes, a crease of worry between her brows. Were they there before? I can't remember. She looks tired, weary, as if life has played some cruel tricks on her and squeezed all the hope and happiness out of her soul. She didn't look like that before we lived in London, I know that much.

'Jake?' she whispers. 'I've been worried sick.'

'I messaged you,' I argue. 'I told you I was safe.'

'Oh, Jake,' Mum says. She holds out her arms and I fall into them, my head on her shoulder. Isla and Maisie snuggle in on the hug, and I pull in a few rough breaths, allow my panic to ebb slowly into acceptance.

'We'll talk about it,' Mum says softly, stroking my hair the way she used to when I was a kid and upset about a nightmare or a cut knee. 'We'll sort it out.'

I used to believe her, back then. Now, not so much.

Paddy and Charlotte come down to join us, and our clumsy embrace disintegrates.

'Mrs Cooke?' Paddy says, offering his hand to shake. 'I think we spoke on the telephone, just after Cookie arrived.'

Mum's eyes widen, and she ignores the offered hand. 'I

don't think so,' she says stiffly. 'I wish you had! I haven't had a clue where Jake was these past few days, and I've certainly never spoken to you before!'

'Cookie?' Paddy says. 'What the heck is going on?'

Charlotte sighs. 'Let's go inside,' she says. 'I think Cookie has some explaining to do.'

We huddle round the kitchen table, sipping hot chocolate and trying to make sense of things. Charlotte has checked Cherry over and found no injuries; she's just grazed and shaken, with bruised wrists where Honey held on to her so tightly. Honey has a few cuts and grazes too, but nothing serious. She and Cherry lean together, as if by touching they can wipe away the hurt and anger of the last few years; suddenly, they don't seem to matter. After all my attempts to get the two of them together, it took an accident to break down the barriers, and show Honey what really mattered.

'Baths and showers for all of you, and then bed,' Charlotte declares, ushering the sisters out of the kitchen. 'We'll talk about this tomorrow, but right now Cookie and his family need some privacy, and what you girls need most of all is sleep.'

❀❀❀❀❀❀❀❀❀❀❀❀❀❀❀❀❀❀❀❀

Charlotte leans down and tucks a blanket round Maisie, curled up and yawning in an armchair next to the Aga with Fred asleep at her feet. Isla is already asleep again, cradled in Mum's arms.

There will be no sleep for me. I shiver a little, still soaked from the thunderstorm, draped in a blanket and cold in spite of the gentle heat of the Aga.

It turns out that Mum looked back through Maisie's texts and found a mention of Kitnor. She grilled Maisie for more information, but all my little sister could remember was my comment about the Chocolate Festival. It wasn't much to go on, but it was something. Mum was determined to find me. They spent half an hour packing up the van, then drove west to Kitnor. The plan was to sleep over in the van and ask the locals for information about the Chocolate Festival in the morning, but they saw a poster on the wall at the end of the lane, spotted the address and found us easily.

Paddy sits down beside me. 'So, Cookie,' he says, 'do you want to explain about the phone call home? Because I think both your mum and I would like to know what happened there.'

I bite my lip. 'I gave you a different mobile number,' I admit. 'I got someone else to talk to you. Pretend to be Mum. I'm sorry, both of you. It was a stupid thing to do. I let you down.'

The kitchen door creaks open again and Honey and Cherry step back into the kitchen, their faces grave. Charlotte rolls her eyes, but my new sisters are not about to be shooed away this time.

'It wasn't Cookie's idea,' Honey says. 'I took his phone and put on a London accent. I thought it was funny to fool you, Paddy. My fault.'

'No, mine.' I argue.

'And I knew, but I didn't tell,' Cherry chips in.

'I'm angry with all three of you,' Paddy says. 'I expected better. I thought I could trust you.'

'You and me both,' Mum says, and shame seeps through my veins like poison. 'Start talking, Jake. I've been beside myself, these last few days. I thought you were at Harry's and I tried to give you space, but something just didn't seem right. And then Mr Zhao showed me the letter you sent and I got really, really scared.'

Isla wakes briefly and gazes at me, her eyes big and

197

solemn; it's one big guilt trip. The guilt twists inside me like a knife, and anger floods into the wound.

I can see Sheddie watching quietly from the sidelines, and I study him quietly. He has gentle brown eyes and looks like he smiles a lot, but I am not fooled. I will not trust him. Mum has always had disastrous taste in men. Sheddie won't be any different.

'What I don't understand is why you came here,' Mum says into the silence. 'I mean, why Somerset? What's the connection? An old school friend?'

I exchange furtive glances with Paddy and Charlotte. 'It's a long story.'

'Better start at the beginning then,' Mum says.

I roll my eyes. 'This is Charlotte Costello,' I announce. 'She used to be Charlotte Tanberry; does that name ring a bell?'

'Charlotte . . . Tanberry?' Mum falters. 'No, I don't think we've met.'

'You haven't met, not exactly,' I explain. 'But you're connected. Because – well, you had an affair with Charlotte's first husband, fifteen years ago. Remember that, Mum? Small world, huh?'

If I'd wanted to lash out at Mum, I couldn't have found a better way to do it. She crumples instantly, her body curling in on itself, shoulders trembling as she covers her face with her hands to hide the tears.

That scares me. Mum hardly ever cries. She has always been the strong one, the fierce, determined one. And now my little sisters are awake and howling too, and Sheddie has stretched an arm round Mum's shoulder. Charlotte is offering her a tissue and Paddy is looking at me sadly as if I am not the boy he thought I was. Disappointment. I have seen that look before, a million times, but even so, it makes me feel bad.

'What Cookie is trying to say is that he came here to meet us,' Honey cuts in. 'His sisters. Is that so wrong? I was staying with Dad in Australia and found out I had a brother; we've been writing for a while. I sent a rail ticket.'

'I didn't plan to use it,' I say. 'But then everything went wrong – the bathtub flood, the ceiling disaster. Mr Zhao blamed me, and he was right; it was my fault. My own stupid fault. You lost your job and we were going to be homeless. Mr Zhao said we had to get out and you said we'd have to move in with Sheddie.'

❀❀❀❀❀❀❀❀❀❀❀❀❀❀❀❀❀❀❀❀❀

'Hang on!' Mum interrupts. 'What are you talking about? I didn't lose my job – I quit. And nobody's pushing us out of the flat; wherever did you get that idea?'

'I overheard you talking to Mr Zhao, the morning after the flood,' I say. 'He was angry. He said we had until Saturday to get out.'

Mum shakes her head. 'No, Jake,' she says gently. 'That morning I told Mr Zhao I was handing in my notice and moving out. Whatever you heard, you got it all wrong. We're not moving in with Sheddie because we've been evicted. Mr Zhao would never do that to us, Jake!'

I frown. What did I actually hear that day? Did I jump to conclusions, add two and two together and come up with five? It wouldn't be the first time. Dismay floods through me.

'But Mr Zhao was so angry,' I argue. 'You said yourself he didn't have the money for repairs, and I knew there was no way we could find that sort of money.'

'But why would we have to?' Mum says. 'It was an accident! The insurers have been round to assess the damage and they're going to pay in full. The restaurant will be good as new – better, actually. And the flat will be too.'

'Insurers?' I echo.

It turns out that Mr Zhao had insurance cover for the restaurant and flat; he paid a yearly fee in case of accidents or emergencies, and now the insurers will pay out for the repairs.

'You said we had to move to Millford, live in a scaffy old yurt . . .'

'Jake, moving in with Sheddie has nothing at all to do with the accident and everything to do with us just wanting to be together,' Mum says. 'We love each other, Jake – it really is that simple.'

I pull a face. I seriously do not want to know about my mum's love life, but I'm baffled at how I can have got things so very wrong. My shoulders slump.

'Your letter really scared me, Jake,' Mum says. 'You told Mr Zhao that you were going to get money . . . How on earth did you plan to do that?'

'Dad,' I say in a sad, small voice. 'I asked Dad. I thought he could talk to Mr Zhao, stop you being thrown out on the streets, maybe pay for the repairs'

'We Skyped him,' Cherry says into the silence. 'An hour or two back. Let's just say it didn't go too well. Cookie ran away and we went after him, and that's when I slipped.'

✿✿✿✿✿✿✿✿✿✿✿✿✿✿✿✿✿✿✿✿

Mum puts her head in her hands. 'You asked Greg?' she says, mortified. 'No way. I don't want his money, Jake! I never have!'

She looks at Charlotte, rakes up a shaky smile. 'I wasn't much more than a kid when I met him,' she explains. 'It was my first job and I hadn't had any serious boyfriends before then. Greg made me feel special. I didn't know he was married, I swear! The romance didn't last; the pregnancy just about finished it off. I lost my job, lost everything, really. He gave me three thousand quid to shut up and stay away. I was naive enough to be pleased at the time, but I'd no clue back then of the cost of bringing up a child. It barely got us through the first year.'

I think of the Skype call, of Greg Tanberry yelling at me that Mum was a gold-digger after his money. The memory still feels raw, like an ache in my gut.

'I didn't realize, Mum,' I say quietly. 'I should have told you where I was going, what I was doing, but I thought you'd try to stop me. It was something I had to do, even if it was a big fat fail. I had all these ideas that Dad would be happy to hear from me, that he'd want to help, want to rescue us – only he wasn't. He wasn't at all . . .'

❀❀❀❀❀❀❀❀❀❀❀❀❀❀❀❀❀❀❀❀❀

Honey steps up beside me and takes my hand in hers, squeezing gently. On my other side, Cherry does the same. I find myself standing straighter, stronger.

'Cookie, I'm so sorry,' Charlotte says. 'Greg is a very flawed man. Selfish, impulsive and never willing to face the consequences of his actions. When I see the mess he's made of other people's lives I sometimes wish I'd never met him, but then I wouldn't have my four lovely daughters, and I wouldn't have Paddy and Cherry. And, of course, your mum wouldn't have you. I don't think either of us would change that for the world.'

'True,' Mum says with a sigh. 'I'd say we both have a lot to be grateful for.'

By the time the sun comes up, things are looking very different.

My little sisters are tucked up on the blue velvet sofas in the living room, fast asleep under soft crocheted blankets. Honey and Cherry have crept away to bed, and as I sneak out of the kitchen door to head back to the caravan to crash out too I reflect on how surreal it is to see Mum and Charlotte holding each other, laughing, talking, crying, and calling each other Alison and Charlotte. As I leave, Paddy and Sheddie are drinking black coffee and discussing fair-trade chocolate and sustainable living and possible t'ai chi workshops for Saturday.

Looks like I'll be staying for the Chocolate Festival after all.

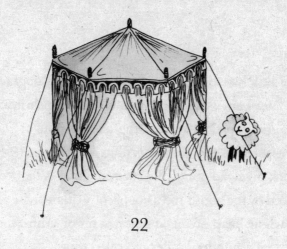

22

When you've stayed up all night to Skype the dad you've never met, had your dreams shattered into a million pieces and run around in a thunderstorm rescuing people from a cliff face – well, you kind of want an easy time the next day. When your mum and little sisters pitch up at three in the morning in a van painted with rainbow stripes and polka dots and CND peace symbols, driven by a crusty bloke with waist-length dreadlocks and the worst name in the world, and everyone sits up until dawn talking about ceilings and insurance and how rubbish my dad was – that's when you really need a lie-in to recover. Until midday at least, or possibly longer.

It doesn't happen.

My mobile says it is 5.50 a.m. when I finally crash out

on the little wooden bunk in the caravan. Roughly three hours later I am woken by the sound of a vehicle crunching across the gravel drive and the klaxon roar of its horn ripping through the quiet morning.

I stick my head out of the caravan door. A flatbed truck is parked by the house and a couple of workmen are unloading a whole heap of metal poles, acres of crimson canvas and about a hundred miles of coiled rope.

I groan. It's Paddy's Indian marquee, arriving too early, too loudly.

I stumble outside and leg it up to the house to talk to the workmen and try to persuade them to carry everything down through the trees to the open grass. By the time I manage that, Paddy and Sheddie have appeared, bleary-eyed and yawning, with Mum, Charlotte and assorted sisters crowding in behind. Everyone grabs a bit of the marquee and we trek down to the bottom of the garden, and one of the workmen gives Paddy a sheet of paper, which is supposed to be the instructions for how to put the wretched thing up. Paddy is still looking slightly stunned and turning the paper upside down to see if it makes more sense that way when we hear the flatbed truck driving away, but Sheddie says that a marquee is not so very different from a yurt, and takes charge of everything.

It is amazing what you can achieve on three hours' sleep, seriously. We slog away for hours putting the frame together, and then reinforcements arrive in the form of Shay, Lawrie and Alfie, and the work goes faster after that. When a couple of vans draw up on the gravel beside the house shortly afterwards, we speculate that it could be more helpers, but actually it turns out to be the TV crew.

'Seriously?' Summer questions. 'They want to film us slogging our guts out? Really?'

'Looks like,' I say. 'I suppose they want to film the run-up to the festival, the preparations.'

'Don't mind us,' Nikki, the clipboard woman, says breezily, as the crew set up their equipment, positioning reflectors and taking sound readings, buzzing around us like flies. 'Pretend we're not here – just act naturally!'

How is anyone supposed to act naturally with that lot breathing down their necks? For the rest of the day, we have to put up with looming cameras and mics that hover above us as we chat, but still, the Indian marquee is taking

✿✿✿✿✿✿✿✿✿✿✿✿✿✿✿✿✿✿✿✿✿

shape and I have almost forgotten that I am blanking Sheddie. Almost, but not quite.

He isn't what I expected. He is quiet and gentle and hard-working, and I can see right away he has Paddy's respect. Mum, Charlotte, Maisie and Isla bring down a picnic feast at lunchtime and we stop to eat and drink. I notice how he looks at Mum and I see the way she glows when she is with him, and I begin to understand that the moving-house thing has nothing at all to do with the bathtub flood and everything to do with how they feel about each other. I see how easy and comfortable my little sisters are with him too – they trust him instinctively. I only wish I could.

'He seems OK,' Cherry says as we eat our sandwiches, shaded from the sun by the half-constructed marquee. 'Sheddie, I mean.'

'Don't be fooled,' I say.

'By what?' Cherry asks. 'By the way he drove all the way to Somerset in the middle of the night to find you? By the way he gets everyone organized and works hard and keeps us all laughing? By the way he is with your mum and your sisters?'

I scowl, checking to make sure no cameras are lurking.

'It's not what I want,' I argue. 'Another disruption, another new start. Millford sounds like a dump. Living in a yurt? No thanks. We had a perfectly good flat.'

'It didn't sound that good,' Cherry comments.

'OK, it was a rubbish flat, but you know what I mean. We don't need him, Cherry. We've managed for two years on our own; it's been fine.'

I look across at Mum and Sheddie, laughing together as the girls jump and swoop around them, chasing Fred, coaxing Humbug the lamb to join in the fun with apple slices and hugs. Maybe we don't need Sheddie, but my mum and my sisters like having him around.

That's where the cameras are, of course, panning out to capture the fun, to tell the story of life at Tanglewood, with bohemian friends pitching in to help organize the festival. If only they knew.

'Was it hard for you to accept Charlotte?' I ask. 'I mean, didn't you ever wish things could stay the way they were, just you and Paddy?'

'I wanted a family,' she says simply. 'I wanted it so badly that sometimes I thought I'd just wished it into being, but

209

it's never been perfect, Cookie. The feud with Honey was the last thing I wanted.'

We look across to where Honey is now holding court for the cameras, the centre of attention, the centre of everything. She sees us watching and waves, picks up a couple of sandwiches and makes her way over. Thankfully, the cameras don't follow.

'I think the feud is over,' I tell Cherry. 'You gave us such a scare. Last night changed everything.'

'I hope so,' Cherry says. 'That's it, though, Cookie, you can change things in a second if you really want to. It's not that difficult. You just have to decide to stop hating, take a chance.'

Maybe.

'Hey!' Honey says. 'Your Sheddie bloke is actually quite cool, isn't he?'

'He's not "my" Sheddie,' I correct her.

Honey shrugs. 'Whatever. I'm just saying. I was telling him what happened last night, how the cliff steps are treacherous when they're wet. And Sheddie said that tomorrow he'll have a go at building another handrail, try to even up the steps, make them less dangerous. Because seriously, guys, last night could have turned out very differently. If you hadn't held on . . .'

'No, if *you* hadn't, Honey,' Cherry says. 'If you hadn't climbed up to rescue me, Cookie – sheesh. Thank you . . . thank you, both. I don't know if I actually said it last night.'

'Only about a million times,' Honey says. 'Don't worry, it was no biggie.'

I look across at Sheddie, wonder if he'd like a hand with the work on the steps tomorrow. Maybe I'll ask.

'How long did it take you to get used to Paddy being your stepdad?' I ask Honey, and she laughs out loud.

'How long?' she echoes. 'Cookie, you do not want to know. I am so, so stubborn. I never like to admit I'm wrong. Well, you know that, Cherry, obviously. But we're OK now, right?'

'Sure,' Cherry says, her cheeks pink with happiness. 'We're good!'

'Give him a chance, Cookie,' Honey says. 'Don't be like I was. What have you got to lose?'

I've lost an awful lot already, as it goes, but I have gained much more, and I have no intention of letting go of my new half-sisters. I have a feeling we will be in each other's lives for a long time.

❁ ❁ ❁ ❁ ❁ ❁ ❁ ❁ ❁ ❁ ❁ ❁ ❁ ❁ ❁ ❁ ❁ ❁ ❁ ❁

We work all afternoon until the marquee is up, looking truly awesome with its tented twin-peaked roof and tasselled trimming and the brightly patterned paisley lining that is hung inside the crimson walls. I hammer in a final tent peg and look up to see Sheddie next to me.

'Nice work, mate,' he says.

'Cheers. Um . . . I was wondering – if you need a hand with the cliff steps tomorrow – well, I'd like to help. But no worries if not.'

Sheddie grins. 'Nice one, kid,' he says. 'I'd appreciate it. Seriously.'

He holds out a hand, tanned and sinewy with a Celtic knot pattern tattooed round the wrist. I reach my hand out too, and we shake, just briefly, and it feels like an understanding, the start of something.

I want to hate Sheddie, I really do, but somehow I just can't.

The next morning we all sleep late. I am woken by Summer knocking on the door of the gypsy caravan, a bundle of letters in her hand.

'I've just come back from walking Fred and I bumped

into the postman – he's amazing at getting letters to places, even when the addresses are a bit wrong!' she tells me with a grin. 'There's a whole pile of stuff for the business, obviously, for Mum and Paddy – and there's one for me. Which is weird, because I never get post – and it's sort of official-looking too. But, anyway, there's one for you as well, Cookie. Here y'go. I hope it's good news!'

'I hope yours is too.'

I watch Summer walk away, the letters in her hand, the dog at her heels. I watch her walk gracefully beneath the trees and up to the house, and once she is out of sight I open my letter.

> JAKE COOKE
> THE CHOCOLATE FESTIVAL PLACE
> KITNOR

DEAR JAKE COOKE,

I WAS VERY CONCERNED TO RECEIVE YOUR RECENT LETTER, AND OF COURSE THE MONEY ENCLOSED. I KNOW YOU WERE UPSET BY THE ACCIDENT, AND I

AM SORRY I TOOK MY TEMPER OUT ON YOU. I HAVE
A SHORT FUSE, COOKIE, BUT I DIDN'T MEAN TO
FRIGHTEN YOU. I KNOW THAT THE FLOOD WAS NOT
YOUR FAULT. TO BE HONEST, I BLAMED MYSELF FOR
NOT GETTING THAT WASHING MACHINE REPAIRED,
FOR PUSHING YOUR MOTHER TO WORK TOO MANY
SHIFTS. I DIDN'T REALLY THINK ABOUT WHO WAS
LOOKING OUT FOR YOUR SISTERS. I WAS SELFISH,
AND I FEEL VERY BAD ABOUT THAT NOW.

THERE WAS NEVER ANY SUGGESTION THAT YOUR
MUM WOULD LOSE HER JOB, COOKIE, NOR YOU
EITHER. AND THERE WAS NEVER EVER ANY CHANCE
THAT YOU WOULD BE PUT OUT ON THE STREETS! AS I
WRITE, THE CEILING IS BEING REPLASTERED. THE
WORKERS HAVE SUGGESTED A FEW EXTRA REPAIRS
THEY CAN DO AT THE SAME TIME, SO ACTUALLY
THINGS ARE WORKING OUT VERY WELL FOR ME. THE
INSURANCE WILL PAY FOR IT ALL, OBVIOUSLY, SO
THERE WAS NO NEED TO SEND ME MONEY.

IF YOUR MUM STILL WANTED HER JOB IT WOULD
BE HERS, BUT SHE IS LEAVING BOTH THE JOB AND
THE FLAT. I AM SORRY TO LOSE HER — IT WILL BE

VERY HARD TO FIND SUCH A GOOD TENANT AND HARD
WORKER. I WILL MISS YOU ALL.

Your mum told me she'd worked out where
you'd gone. I hope she found you, and that you
are still there, because I didn't get the
chance to return your mum's deposit on the
flat. The flat was in a much better state
than when you all moved in, so returning the
deposit is the least I can do. It's £500. I
hope the cheque comes in useful for you in
your new home.

Do call in if you are ever in Chinatown,
and may good fortune follow you all.

Your good friend,
Deshi Zhao

23

I hand the cheque to Mum at breakfast, all of us squashed round the big kitchen table at Tanglewood. The cheque means all kinds of things: friendship, forgiveness, fairness, a future. It's quite something. We are toasting Mr Zhao with orange juice when Summer comes in, her eyes starred with tears.

'What's wrong, sweetheart?' Charlotte asks, jumping up. 'Has something happened?'

Summer takes a deep breath and holds out a sheet of headed notepaper, her hand shaking. Skye takes it, her eyes widening. 'Oh wow!' she says.

It turns out that Summer's letter is quite something too. Her dance teacher has recommended her for a teaching scholarship at the boarding ballet school she once auditioned at. The principal has written to offer her a place, starting in September.

'I didn't even know they did teaching scholarships,' she says breathlessly. 'Can you imagine? They'll train me to teach, not to perform, so no pressure. Sylvie Rochelle says that I have a huge talent and a rare gift for inspiring others, that she wants me to be part of the team.'

There is so much hugging then that breakfast is forgotten, and Paddy uncorks a bottle of fizzy wine and tops up everyone's orange juice with a little dash of that, and Maisie and Isla cling on to Summer and ask if she'll teach them to dance. She promises she will.

Mum and Sheddie watch it all with interest; they don't know why this means so much to Summer, how close she came to achieving her dream, how cruelly she lost it. Can they guess, looking at the slender arms thrown tightly round her twin, how fragile she has been, how strong she is inside to have come through it? Maybe.

'What's the story with the sad-eyed girl?' Sheddie asks later, as we work together on the cliff steps. 'Summer, right?'

'Eating disorder,' I say quietly, hammering in one of the

wooden stakes we cut earlier to make the new handrails. 'She's lots better now, apparently, but a couple of years ago she was really ill. She wanted to be a dancer, and now it looks like she'll be a teacher instead, but I think that's OK. I think she's happy.'

'I think so too,' Sheddie says. 'Doing something you love – finding your happy thing – is worth a whole lot, even if it doesn't make you rich and famous. For your mum, it's yoga and reflexology; she'll get to do all that stuff again when we live in Millford. Make a little business of it, maybe.'

'Huh.' I move away from Sheddie, further up the steps, start hammering in a new upright. I do not want to talk about Millford. I am not ready to cave in, be best mates with Sheddie, buy into the future he wants to map out for us. I know I don't have a choice about Millford, not any more, but I need to take things slowly, get my head round it.

Earlier on we pressed fine chicken wire so tightly round the ragged steps that it made our fingers bleed, but at least now when it rains again, it will offer some grip. Then we spent hours in the scrubby woodland that edges the beach, cutting armfuls of strong branches from the hazel trees that grow wild there. Now, with all the uprights in, Sheddie gets

❀❀❀❀❀❀❀❀❀❀❀❀❀❀❀❀❀❀

me to hold the long, twisty branches on top while he nails them into position to create new handrails that are beautiful as well as sturdy.

When the steps are finished, every muscle in my body aches, but I'm proud of what we've done. While I dump the offcuts next to the half-built after-party bonfire and gather up the tools, Sheddie adds the last touch: solar-powered fairy lights threaded all along the handrails. Now the steps will be safer at night too.

It looks amazing.

We walk together back up to the house, past the Indian marquee now filled with tables and chairs borrowed from one of the local village halls, bright with red chequered tablecloths and jam-jar vases filled with garden flowers, under treetops heavy with yet more fairy lights, and past the brightly painted stage now adorned with banners and bunting. Trestle tables are positioned round the edges of the garden, ready to be transformed in the morning into the various stalls. It looks like everyone has been busy today.

'D'you ever think about what your happy thing might be, Cookie?' Sheddie asks as we put the tools away in the stable storeroom. 'Any ideas?'

❀❀❀❀❀❀❀❀❀❀❀❀❀❀❀❀❀❀❀❀❀❀

I think that being with my sisters, both the big ones and the little ones, makes me happy. I think that the countryside and the ocean and the dark sky at night studded with stars makes me happy too, and those are things I never expected. I even think that working hard to make something, do something, makes me feel good, like building the stage and fixing the cliff steps.

I'm not sure those are the kind of things Sheddie means, though.

'Not a clue,' I say with a shrug. 'I've never really thought about it before. What about you, Sheddie? What's your happy thing?'

He looks at me for a moment, a little wary. 'You want the truth?' he asks. 'It's your mum, Cookie. Simple as that.'

Back at the caravan, I check my emails one last time; nothing from Dad. It's not a surprise, but still, it makes me sad. There are so many things we could have said, could have done. I tried to reach out, build a bridge, but Dad blew it right out from under my feet. There's nothing left to salvage.

Even so, I find myself typing one last email.

❀❀❀❀❀❀❀❀❀❀❀❀❀❀❀❀❀❀❀❀❀❀❀

Dear Dad,

I'd like to say it was cool to Skype you the other day, but both of us know that wouldn't be the truth. I guess I'd built you up in my mind to be some kind of hero figure, and when you turned out to be more of a villain, it kind of did my head in.

You will be glad to know that I didn't need your help or your money in the end – everything has turned out a lot better than I imagined it would and no cash for emergency repairs was needed. Which is just as well, as there's no way on earth you'd have coughed up. That's OK – you keep your money. I hope it keeps you warm at night.

So, yeah, I've missed you all these years without even being aware of it, and in the end it turns out I was better off without you – who knew? I have the most amazing mum ever. It's sad that you can't see that, but hey, your loss. I have two brilliant little half-sisters and now a bunch of new ones too, and a whole lot of other people who look like being fairly awesome. I've had the best ever time at Tanglewood and I've learnt a lot – and the biggest lesson of all has been that running away doesn't solve your problems, it only adds to them. The way to sort things out is to get the

❁ ❁

facts, ask for help, work with others to fix things up.

Thing is, Dad, you seem to be pretty good at the running-away thing yourself. You had the perfect set-up at Tanglewood. A beautiful house, a cool wife, four cute daughters who loved you – and you threw it all away like so much rubbish, just like you threw my mum away, and me. It's like you're looking for some mythical perfect life with a fast car and champagne for breakfast every day.

Well, I hope you find it, Dad, and I hope it makes you happy. I hope you don't wake up one day all lost and lonely and suss that happiness is not about how much you own but about the people you have in your life and the love that binds you all together. The stuff that makes you rich – well, it's got nothing to do with money.

Life is an adventure, and mine hasn't always been easy – but still, I wouldn't change a bit of it. I wish you luck, Dad, and happiness. I won't be emailing again.

Jake Cooke

24

Saturday dawns bright and clear, and we're up before seven, putting the finishing touches in place. Honey drapes the trestle tables with sari fabric, and sets out a series of hand-painted signs for the stalls and sideshows.

I head down through the trees to tug the tarpaulin coverings from the handmade stage. They fall away, revealing the blue painted wood with its stars and crescent moons, the branches holding the painted backdrop, which declares *Tanglewood Chocolate Festival*, and the carefully woven driftwood arch with fairy lights threaded through it. I know I have created something amazing, something to be proud of.

'You did this?' Sheddie asks, something like pride in his voice. 'It's quite something, Cookie. You've got some skill in those hands, d'you know that?'

'Cheers, man,' I say.

'It's incredible,' Paddy agrees. 'You're a bit of a dark horse, Jake Cooke! This is going to be the focal point of the whole festival. Thank you!'

My heart swells. I don't know if I've ever had a better compliment. I hope the stage says thank you right back to Paddy and the others more eloquently than I ever could with words. I have to hope that it does.

Shay and Alfie arrive and start setting up the sound system, turning the stage into something functional, something more amazing still; blasts of indie pop blare out at random intervals, scaring passers-by down on the beach who are quietly walking their dogs.

Coco has turned the duck pond enclosure into a miniature petting zoo. Humbug the sheep mingles with the runner ducks and attempts to paddle in the water, while Lawrie's three-legged fox, Bracken, snuggles up in her own pen alongside. Coco and Lawrie's stall is all about wildlife and global warming and saving the giant panda, and later on they will offer pony rides round the field next door to raise money for a local animal sanctuary. A corner of the same field has been set aside for t'ai chi workshops, and Mum has made a canopied bower underneath the trees and set up a sign announcing reflexology treatments.

As for Maisie and Isla, thanks to Skye they are kitted out in brown and gold net and home-made fairy wings, the littlest of chocolate fairies with satin ballet shoes on their feet and brown and gold ribbons tumbling from their hair. My other sisters look amazing too, other-worldly in their brown velvet vest tops and net-and-ribbon tutu skirts, cheekbones shimmering with fairy dust, peacock-bright fairy wings bobbing as they walk.

'There was some talk of making us boys dress up too,' Alfie tells me darkly. 'Skye mentioned something about brown skinny jeans and little hats with feathers. I told her, over my dead body!'

'Phew,' I grin. 'Good work, Alfie!'

Alfie will be running the car park, a field opposite the gate to Tanglewood; the gravel drive is reserved for family, us included, and for the TV crew. Shay is running the music part of the festival, with a talent show for the children as well as slots from several local bands and his own solo set. Skye has taken over the gypsy caravan, transforming it; she plans to sit on the steps, telling chocolate fortunes. Cherry, Charlotte and Paddy are running the Chocolate Box stall, the most important part of the whole festival, and Sandy, Lawrie's mum, will be in charge of the kitchen, sending out orders for the chocolate cafe in the Indian marquee. Honey, Summer, Millie and Tia will be acting as waitresses; the chocolate cafe sold out at the last chocolate festival, apparently, and all week the sisters have been helping Charlotte to bake an array of mouth-watering cakes.

And now the other stallholders are arriving too: a woman from the village who is running a cake-decorating stall, a couple of Coco's friends who are manning the chocolate taste test stall, someone running workshops on making fairy wings, face painters, people running charity stalls and even a kids' dressing-up area run by the little museum in Kitnor, complete with a fun photo booth attached.

The TV crew are here already, doing vox pops with some of the stallholders, asking Paddy and Charlotte to say a few words about what makes The Chocolate Box so special. Suddenly in the spotlight, Paddy shrugs and leads the crew down to the stage; it's the perfect backdrop for his speech.

❀❀❀❀❀❀❀❀❀❀❀❀❀❀❀❀❀❀❀❀❀❀

'What is The Chocolate Box about?' he asks. 'It's about a dream, I guess. It's about wanting to do something and making it happen, against all the odds, against all advice. It's about teamwork – working together, friends and family, making our products as good as they possibly can be. Our truffles are sweet and rich and gorgeous, but they're more than that. They're fairly traded and handmade with love. And you can't beat that, really, can you?'

The camera turns to Charlotte, and she picks up a box of Paddy's newly created truffles. 'Paddy's said it all,' she says. 'But he hasn't told you about the hard work, the long hours, the planning and creativity. And he hasn't told you about our newest creation, our Fortune Cookie truffle! It's exclusive to the festival today, but we're hoping to roll it out to all our suppliers in the coming weeks – let's just say it's chocolate with a heart!'

And then Nikki, the clipboard woman, is ushering the sisters into the shot, pushing forward Sandy and Lawrie and Shay and Alfie, finally even Mum, Sheddie, Maisie, Isla and me. Everyone is grinning like mad, squashed together, happy, standing under the driftwood arch with the fairy lights twinkling.

❁❁❁❁❁❁❁❁❁❁❁❁❁❁❁❁❁❁❁

'Teamwork,' Paddy says again. 'That's what we do, and every truffle is a little bit of magic!'

'Cut!' Nikki says. 'Fabulous! I suspect things will be too busy later for anything like that, so I wanted to get it in early – and what a setting. Visually gorgeous! Now, time's ticking on. Ten minutes till opening!'

'Will people come, d'you think?' I ask Honey. 'Will it be OK?'

'There are cars lined up in the lane already,' she points out. 'They'll come, trust me. How did it go with Sheddie yesterday? OK?'

'Yeah, OK,' I admit. 'How about you? Any word from Ash?'

She pulls a face. 'I've pretty much given up on that,' she says. 'No worries. I'll get over it.'

'Kids?' Paddy yells. 'Everyone get to your places; gates open in five minutes. Thank you and good luck!'

I'm taking first shift on the gate, collecting the £1 entry fee and handing out a little leaflet with a map of Tanglewood and a list of all the stalls and activities available. I have a cash tin with a £20 float and a little rubber stamp with 'Chocolate Festival' on it so I can stamp people's hands as they come in to prove that they've paid. It's a responsible job, I kid you not.

Honey and I exchange glances and head off in opposite directions, grinning. I'm just about ready when Paddy strides up to open the gate. The first few visitors arrive in a trickle, and it's easy enough to take their money and stamp their hands and give out leaflets. Then somehow there's a queue in the lane and I am scrabbling for change and forgetting to stamp hands and dropping leaflets on the floor; it's just too crazy. I've lost count, but I know for sure that hundreds of people have trekked in through this gate, and when I look up and across the lane I see row upon row of parked cars in Alfie's car park field.

In the distance, I hear Shay announcing the children's talent show over the sound system, and for the next hour there's a soundtrack of reedy singing and dodgy uke playing and some fairly awesome compering from Shay. The TV crew are right in the thick of it, interviewing the festival-goers, chatting to people queuing to buy chocolate, to have their fortunes told, to do a t'ai chi class, have a reflexology treatment. The Indian marquee is full to bursting, the waitresses running up and down with trays

❀❀❀❀❀❀❀❀❀❀❀❀❀❀❀❀❀❀❀❀❀

laden with milkshakes, ice-cream sundaes, cupcakes and chocolate fudge cake. Kids skip past with their faces painted, dressed as Victorians or wearing home-made fairy wings fashioned out of willow and tissue paper. Everyone is smiling.

Out of nowhere, Cherry appears at my side. 'Coping?' she asks. 'It's manic, isn't it? We've sold out of Dad's new Fortune Cookie truffles already; people are loving them! We're taking orders for them now!'

'Crazy here too,' I say. 'Just so many people! It's calmed down a little bit now, but they're still coming. It's mad!'

As I speak, another punter comes through the gate, a tall, slim boy with blue-black hair and skin the colour of coffee. He has a huge backpack and hefts it down on to the ground as he roots in a pocket for change.

'Hey,' he says in a broad Aussie accent. 'I'm looking for a girl called Honey Tanberry. She around?'

Cherry's eyes widen. 'Hang on . . . are you Ash?' she says. 'Oh wow! You certainly chose your moment!'

'I didn't choose it, the TV people did,' he says with a grin. 'They've been in touch with me for weeks, trying to arrange this. Highlight of their reality TV show, apparently.'

❀❀❀❀❀❀❀❀❀❀❀❀❀❀❀❀❀❀❀❀

'No way,' I breathe. 'This is all a set-up? Honey's been going crazy because she hasn't heard from you for a week. She thought you'd dumped her!'

'I wasn't allowed to text,' Ash says, 'in case it spoiled the surprise. She's probably furious with me, but that was the deal. They paid my train fares and I had to keep quiet.'

'She's been really worried,' I tell him. 'But I have a feeling it'll all be forgotten once she sees you! Can you look after the gate, Cherry? C'mon, Ash, I'll help you find her!'

The TV crew spot us at once as we make our way through the crowds towards the chocolate cafe; a camera follows us to the doorway. 'Can you just stand and gaze out across the marquee?' the cameraman asks. 'I'll do a close-up and then a sweeping shot of the cafe.'

Ash just laughs, grinning at the camera before glancing out across the crowds, his face hopeful.

Honey is serving tea and cake to two middle-aged ladies when she looks up and sees him for the first time. Her easy chat crashes to a halt and the teacup slides out of her hand and on to the ground.

'Ash?' she whispers. 'Ash, seriously? Oh. My. God!'

She runs at him and jumps into his arms, almost knocking him over, and the two of them are laughing and hugging and whirling round and round on the grass as the cameras film it all.

25

It is all beyond perfect in the end, and the TV crew capture everything. I don't know much about film or editing, but I know that in the weeks to come they will be able to cut and edit the footage together to make something amazing. It's reality TV with a soul, a sweet story to warm the hearts of the viewers in the cold autumn nights to come.

They'll love every bit: the blended family, the dramas and friendships and the cool, quirky, bohemian sisters with their hopes and dreams and friends and boyfriends. All this is set against a background of stunning Exmoor countryside, the beach, the sea, the house – oh, and the chocolate. Yeah. Call me a cynic if you like, but I think the TV show will be a hit, and if the show is a hit the business will be too.

Nikki, the clipboard woman who has been running the show, certainly seems to think so. She's a friend of Paddy and Charlotte's, the mother of Skye's ex-boyfriend Finch. Now that the festival is over and the cameras have gone, she puts down her clipboard and sits with us round a make-shift driftwood bonfire on the beach. We've cleared away the worst of the mess, stacked plates, filled the dishwasher; now, for a little while at least, there is nothing to do but chill.

We go over and over the day's events. For once, Honey looks almost shy, her face shining with happiness.

'Ash is just the most awesome person I know,' she says simply. 'Apart from you guys, obviously. Can you believe he's just travelled across Europe to surprise me? How cool is that? Although I am not sure if I can ever forgive him for not texting me. Boy, are you in trouble!'

Ash just laughs, leaning into her, his fingers twined round hers.

'Your new truffle was a huge hit,' Nikki comments. 'The one with the little chocolate message inside. What was it called? Fortune Cookie?'

'Named after this young man,' Charlotte says, grinning

❀❀❀❀❀❀❀❀❀❀❀❀❀❀❀❀❀❀❀❀❀❀❀❀

at me. 'So, what kind of future do you see for us, Cookie? Any predictions?'

I roll my eyes. 'Well, you and Paddy are going to be household names soon, of course,' I declare. 'The reality TV show will see to that. Not only will The Chocolate Box be the UK's favourite chocolate brand, it'll change the whole industry for the better – more and more chocolate firms will become fair trade and organic. Fame and fortune and happiness, how about that?'

'Sounds good to me,' Paddy laughs. 'How about the girls?'

'Yeah, how about us?' Honey chimes in, grinning. 'Can I have some fame and fortune too?'

'Well, you're definitely going to be famous, Honey,' I tell her. 'A famous artist. I'm not sure if you'll be rich, but so what? You'll live with Ash in an attic apartment in Paris, and eat *pain au chocolat* for breakfast and paint all day and go dancing at night, and Ash will write research papers on – I dunno – philosophy or something. Summer's going to be a dance teacher, we know that already; she'll train some of the country's most famous ballerinas, and one day she'll take over that fancy boarding ballet school – what is it called?'

'Rochelle Academy,' Summer says, breathless. 'Wow. I wish!'

'It'll happen,' I promise. 'And Alfie will do the cooking and the paperwork, and you'll have three or four kids, all girls, all awesome at dancing.'

Alfie howls with laughter and tries to elbow me in the ribs, but I can tell he's pleased. I look up, notice Isla twirling round and round on the sand, her fairy wings juggling, ribbons flying out as she moves.

'Skye, you're going to be a highly acclaimed costume designer,' I say. 'You'll style and dress world-famous actors for award-winning films and TV series. And you'll go on wearing vintage till you're old and grey.'

Skye laughs, and I move on to Cherry. 'You'll be a writer, clearly,' I say. 'You'll start off in journalism and write a children's book in your spare time about a girl called Sakura. The book will take off and turn into a series, and then a film. Trust me, you'll end up richer than Shay, and everyone knows he's going to be a superstar.'

'What about me?' Coco asks, pouting. 'Will I save the world? Or run my own animal rescue? Or end up working in Tesco's?'

'You'll go to uni to study to be a vet,' I tell her. 'You'll get the best grades in your class, but in your final year you'll join Greenpeace and drop out of uni to sail to the Arctic on that boat – what's it called? *Rainbow Warrior*. You'll set up a sanctuary for polar bears and years later you'll marry your childhood sweetheart, Lawrie.'

Coco blushes crimson and Lawrie looks horrified, but the others are shrieking with laughter. 'Go on – go on . . . how many children?' they want to know. 'How many three-legged foxes?'

I shake my head. 'No kids,' I decree. 'Coco's going to go into politics and will end up becoming Britain's first eco-prime minister. She really will save the world, or our little corner of it. And I'll be able to say I knew her before she was famous.'

'Yessss!' Coco crows. 'My fortune's the best – love it, Cookie! I wonder if it'll happen. I wonder if any of it will?'

I wink at her. 'Wait and see,' I tease.

Honey snakes an arm round my shoulder, sighing. 'I am going to miss you *so* much, little brother,' she says. 'I don't want you to go. It's not fair. We've only really just found you, and now we're losing you again.'

'You won't lose me,' I argue. 'Not ever. We're all part of the same jigsaw, right?'

'Definitely,' Cherry agrees. 'We should arrange to meet up every year here at Tanglewood, on the beach, with a bonfire burning and guitars playing, until we're old and ancient. That way we'll never lose touch.'

'That's a deal,' I say.

We sit round the bonfire until the light begins to fade and Paddy gets up to light the jam-jar lanterns hanging from hooks skewered into the damp sand. Shay plays guitar and Paddy joins in on the fiddle for a while, and then Coco does, and even though her playing makes my ears hurt, I can't help smiling.

It's almost eleven by the time Mum and Sheddie creep away to put Maisie and Isla to bed. 'Don't be too late, Jake,' Mum warns me. 'We're setting off early in the morning, remember; it's a long drive to Millford.'

That brings me back down to earth all right.

The party breaks up slowly after that; we're beyond tired, but happy too. Paddy and Charlotte and Sandy and Nikki head back up to the house; the sisters and their friends wander up to the marquee, where a summer sleep-out

❀❀❀❀❀❀❀❀❀❀❀❀❀❀❀❀❀❀❀❀❀❀

among the remnants of the chocolate cafe has been planned.

Me, I just want to be alone for a little while.

The bonfire burns down to embers and the light is falling fast. I sit on the beach for another hour or so as the sky darkens to the colour of blue-black ink, watching the stars come out one by one beneath a perfect sliver of moon.

Mum knocks at the door or the gypsy caravan at six, and ten minutes later I am washed and dressed, eating leftover pizza slices in the Tanglewood kitchen. Sheddie's van is packed and ready, and Mum lifts my little sisters up into the back seats and fastens their seatbelts.

There are supposed to be no goodbyes, no tears, no regrets. All our farewells have already been made, at the bonfire party last night, but Paddy and Charlotte come out on to the gravel for more hugs, more promises to keep in touch.

'I saved you some of those new truffles,' Paddy says, handing me a small patterned box tied up with ribbon. 'The Fortune Cookie ones, there's one each. The TV

❀❀❀❀❀❀❀❀❀❀❀❀❀❀❀❀❀❀❀❀❀❀❀

people reckon they're going to be a bestseller, and if they are, Cookie, I'll have you to thank!'

And then we're in the van – Mum and Sheddie up front, me in the back next to Maisie and Isla – and Sheddie fires up the engine and the van crawls across the gravel towards the gate.

'*Cookie!*' someone calls, and I look out of the window to see Honey and Cherry running up through the trees, the twins and Coco behind them. Five crumpled and sleepy chocolate fairies are lined up on the five-bar gate, waving, as Sheddie turns the van out on to the road.

'Good luck in Millford!' Cherry yells. 'Don't forget us!'

'Write to me!' Honey adds. 'Come back soon!'

And then we drive over the brow of the hill, and Tanglewood is gone behind us, fading already into memory. For a while we can see the sea, a blue-grey smudge in the distance, and then that is gone too, as if it had never been there at all.

'What are these chocolates then?' Mum asks.

'It's just something Paddy does,' I explain. 'He's created truffles for all the sisters, and he made one for me too. Fortune Cookie, he's called it, and every one has a prediction hidden inside. They sold out at the Chocolate Festival yesterday.'

'Nice idea,' Mum says. 'What are they like?'

I offer the truffles round, and everybody takes one.

'Yummy!' Maisie declares, biting into the truffle. 'Oh, what's this inside?'

She pulls out a chocolate heart with the words, 'Dream big' engraved on it.

'Ooh I get it now,' she says. 'Chocolate fortunes!'

Isla's fortune says, 'Happy families', Mum's says, 'Take a risk', and Sheddie's says, 'New beginnings'. They are good fortunes, hopeful fortunes.

'Now you,' Maisie says, and I reach for the last truffle in the box, bite into the rich ganache until my teeth touch the chocolate heart within.

'Soon life will become more interesting,' it says in tiny writing, and I laugh out loud.

I think this time it really might.

Catch all the latest
news and gossip from

Cathy Cassidy

at

www.cathycassidy.com

- ★ Sneaky peeks at new titles
- ★ Details of signings and events near you
- ★ Audio extracts and interviews with Cathy
- ★ Post your messages and pictures

Don't Miss a Word!

Sign up to receive a FREE email newsletter
from Cathy in your inbox every month!
Go to *www.cathycassidy.com*

Which Chocolate Box Girl Are You?

Your perfect day would be spent . . .
a) visiting a busy vintage market
b) with your favourite canine companion on a long walk in the countryside
c) curled up on the sofa watching black-and-white movies with your boyfriend
d) window-shopping with your BFF
e) sipping frappuccinos in a hip city cafe

Your ideal boy is . . .
a) arty and sensitive
b) boy? No thanks!
c) a good listener . . . and a little bit quirky
d) polite and clever
e) good looking and popular – what other kind of boy is there?

Who's the first person you would tell about your new crush?
a) your sister – she knows everything about you
b) your pet cat . . . animals are great listeners
c) your BFF
d) your mum – she always has the best advice
e) no one. It's best not to trust anyone with a secret

Your favourite subject is . . .
a) history
b) science
c) creative writing
d) French
e) drama

Your school books are . . .
a) covered in paisley-print fabric
b) a bit muddy
c) filled with doodles
d) neat, tidy and full of good grades
e) rarely handed in on time

When you grow up you want to be . . .

a) an interior designer
b) a vet
c) a writer
d) a prima ballerina
e) famous

People always compliment your . . .

a) individuality. If anyone can pull it off you can!
b) caring nature – every creature deserves a bit of love
c) wild imagination . . . although it can get you into trouble sometimes
d) determination. Practice makes perfect
e) strong personality. You never let anyone stand in your way

Mostly As . . . *Skye*

Cool and eclectic, friends love your relaxed boho style and passion
for all things quirky.

Mostly Bs . . . *Coco*

A real mother earth, but with your feet firmly on the ground, you're
happiest in the great outdoors – accompanied by a whole menagerie
of animal companions.

Mostly Cs . . . *Cherry*

'Daydreamer' is your middle name . . . Forever thinking up crazy stories and
buzzing with new ideas, you always have an exciting tale to tell – you're
allowed a bit of artistic licence, right?

Mostly Ds . . . *Summer*

Passionate and fun, you're determined to make your dreams come
true . . . and your family and friends are behind you every step of the way.

Mostly Es . . . *Honey*

Popular, intimidating, lonely . . . everyone has a different idea about the
'real you'. Try opening up a bit more and you'll realize that friends are there
to help you along the way.

Yummy Ice-cream Sundaes

Banana Split

You need:

1 banana
vanilla ice cream
chopped nuts
chocolate sauce

Method:
Slice the banana in half lengthways, place in a dish and arrange three scoops of vanilla ice cream between the halves.

Decorate with a sprinkle of chopped nuts and a squoosh of chocolate sauce!

Chocolate Heaven

You need:
3 chocolate chip cookies, crumbled
4 squares chocolate, grated
vanilla ice cream
chocolate ice cream
chocolate sauce
aerosol cream

Method:
In a tall glass, layer a scoop of vanilla ice cream, a sprinkle of crumbled cookie, a scoop of chocolate ice cream and a layer of grated chocolate, and another scoop of vanilla ice cream and a layer of crumbled cookie. Top with a layer of squishy aerosol cream and decorate with grated chocolate and sauce . . . bliss!

Strawberry Sundae

You need:

fresh strawberries
plain frozen yoghurt
strawberry yoghurt
strawberry sauce

Method:
Cut most of the fresh strawberries into quarters then layer in a tall glass with the plain frozen yoghurt, strawberry yoghurt and an occasional squirt of strawberry sauce.

Repeat the layers until you reach the top of the glass. Finish off with the leftover strawberries and an extra squoosh of strawberry sauce!

Welcome inside the world of the chocolate box girls

Cathy Cassidy

the chocolate box Secrets

Perfect presents and cool fashion for all year round...

A *delicious* scrapbook of fun, creative ideas from **Cherry, Summer, Skye, Coco** and **Honey.**

- *Host* a chocolate-themed sleepover
- *Design* a flower headband
- *Create* a cupcake sensation

And many more ideas for every season

A whole year of **Chocolate-Box-inspired ideas** – which one will you make first?